TROMBONES
CAN LAUGH

To Jeff.

Trombones Can Laugh

Lorraine Ray

CHAPTER ONE

I was living in Parental Weirdsville, U.S.A. on the night my old man asked me if I wanted to play the trombone.

Everything had been groovy until his knock. Shoot, it had been stunningly cool, laid back, and I was contemplating a fine evening of model-making.

My old man's appearance at my bedroom door was the pits. I knew it was him, and I was freaking out; ordinarily the old man obeyed the call of his pipe and his drafting table heaped with building plans, mechanical pencils, and plastic templates of teeny little toilets. Mechanical engineering stuff. The tools of his trade. He made it a habit to stay till midnight in our converted garage, rum and coke bubbling away in a large blue hand-blown tumbler from Mexico, the TV blaring anything western followed by *The Tonight Show*.

Shoot, the pipe smoke used to stack up in hazy blue layers until it was a few feet above the damn carpet. If he ever took a break, it was to go outside and stare up at the stars.

Wow, I thought that night, what the hell was he doing at my door? Why the hassle? Why the visit? My fingers trembled as I spun the cap onto the tube of plastic cement. I crossed the threads. I remember seeing the cap sitting catawampus on the tube when my damn door creaked open.

The old man's square face worked its way in. A high wave of Bryl Creemed hair (more than a little dab) and browline glasses. He found his twelve-year-old son, crouching at a small pine desk under a crook-necked lamp, having just slathered an enormous quantity of plastic cement on the halves of the fuselage of a

Sopwith Camel biplane. The top of my desk was littered with tiny tubes of the glue, with glass bottles of enamel paint, and with poorly assembled models of the Rat Fink Hot Rod Series. Let me see, there was Mr. Gasser, Drag Nut, Endsville Eddie and Weird-oh. I'd built them all—poorly. Earlier that evening, I'd slopped paint all over the helmet and vampire teeth of Drag Nut, using a new, red, metal-flake enamel.

And then, high on glue and paint fumes, I lifted my head to hear my old man ask me, "James, don't you think the glue smell is awfully strong in here?"

"Huh," I said, blinking twice at him like some drugged owl.

He repeated his question.

"No, sir," I said.

"You're straining your lungs to find any air," he warned.

"No sweat, Dad. I can breathe."

"Well...let's air this room out. It might be dangerous. Explosive. And while we're doing that let me show you some photos. They're of my band and me. When I played trombone. We're—"

"One moment, Dad. I'm gluing," I said, holding a palm up at him. Always postpone the Inevitable and Unavoidable Parental Weirdness for as long as you can, I remember thinking.

He waited patiently while I, behind my coke-bottle thick glasses, pressed the fuselage firmly together. I'd have to pry it apart later that night. Shoot, I was doing precisely the wrong step—number 25 in the circle instead of number 24. Perhaps he guessed this. (How in hell was I going to get the wings on when the fuselage had already been glued together?) His face did express disappointment at the messy smear of plastic cement I'd created when the fuselage went together. Like the Rat Fink models, this airplane would be a klutzy disaster, the plastic actually melting from the enormous amount of cement I slathered indiscriminately everywhere. Damn, I was a real ding-a-ling when I was a kid. Hey, who am I kidding? I still am.

I emerged eventually.

"I was having a ball," the old man said awkwardly, trying to use my favorite idiom at the time, "I think you'll be interested in what I did. Back then, I was always having a ball playing the trombone."

As I said, I was a dumb little fellow, and I did believe he'd once "had a ball." I made it a rule not to protest too much about things that happened to me, or about being told what to do, so naturally I left the Sopwith fuselage and my delicious glue and went along. Cheerfully. The old man's hand on my shoulder, across the hall a few steps to the family living room.

Our family of five shared a little ranch-styled brick home. Imagine this suburban 1960s Arizona horror with dark brown linoleum tiles infecting every floor and veneered Danish modern furniture dropped here and there in front of drippy watercolors of New York skyscrapers. Arranged on the Danish modern furniture, it was possible to find five or six orange triangular plastic ashtrays for my father who smoked like some Beatnik dragon. The New York watercolors were there because my mother liked pretending she was a sophisticated person from Indiana who knew a lot about New York and had just landed in Southern Arizona by accident because of the attractive winter weather.

I sat on the sofa where the old man put me. He left me there and crossed the room to the stereo hi-fi where he dropped the needle on his favorite album which happened to be Tijuana Brass' *South of the Border*. My old man did not pretend to be sophisticated. No siree. An engineer could never carry that off when he worked in an office full of architects. Those guys were always skiing in the mountains of Idaho, wrecking English sports cars, and having affairs with their big-boobed secretaries. My old man just didn't have any of that in him. I guess I'm kinda thankful for that; who would be happy about a dad who did crap like that? English sports cars are special things and you shouldn't wreck them! Anyway, as I was saying, after he dropped the needle on the album, he knelt down in front of a cabinet behind the sofa where we kept our family photo albums.

"Ah," he said, sliding out this old black and white picture

album of his. It had black paper pages and white writing underneath. The photos were smaller than the photos today. A very weird, dusty old thing. My old man plopped the album on my lap. And opened it.

"Me at the ranch," he said sternly.

I put my face closer to the album to see it properly. I noticed he was out in a dry field. Evenly spaced bushes stretching off into a dusty horizon made up of low mountains. The bushes were cotton, I thought. I'd seen tons of that junk, Arizona is crawling with it, and practically the whole country is snoozing on Pima cotton, but they're too dumb to realize it. We got the strain from the local Natives around here. Hell, I guess Americans don't care about agricultural facts any more than I do.

"I fainted shortly after my uncle took that picture. In the cotton fields in Avra Valley. I was driving the tractor myself. It was one hundred and five degrees out that day. I blacked out completely, but," my old man remembered what he was supposed to be showing me, "I wanted you to see pictures of me in the band." He flipped to another page and the brittle black paper scraped the end of my nose and brushed me back.

Next, my old man pointed out a picture of himself with the coronet. "My first instrument was the coronet. It's like a trumpet, but it doesn't play as many notes."

I let my face fall close to the page again, so that I could see real good and really dig this time of his life. "I started playing the coronet in junior high, because my mother had an old one of those, but then I decided the trombone played more notes. I thought shooting that old brass slide out would be fun, too. Swing, I was crazy for that stuff. The trombone was a lot jazzier."

Another photo showed him where he was standing beside a thick wooden surfboard in San Diego. "We used to drive over to San Diego. Always at night, 'cause it was cooler. Mother and sis and I drove over there together. I liked to surf."

"Here I am at the Navy Station in San Diego. Training."

He still hadn't gotten to his crazy adventures in the swing

band before he went into the Navy. You see, he'd flipped too deeply into the album and had to work his way back.

"Ah, here. Here I was at the Naval Station north of Chicago. I was a pecker checker, James. All because I was a wise guy and shot off my mouth at some higher up. Let that be a lesson to you. A pecker checker had the delightful job of checking the penises of men who were enlisting in the Navy to see if the guys had V.D. I kid you not. And later, when the war was almost over, I took care of nuts-o Marines in the crazy asylum. I wrestled them into straightjackets. All of this happened north of Chicago. When I went to Chicago (this picture, here) the damned USO only served me hot dogs for breakfast, lunch and dinner. You notice I don't eat those damn things anymore."

"Yeah, you sure don't like em," I chipped in.

"That's right. A pecker checker. And I got served hot dogs for every meal. Do you see a tie-in?" he said raising an eyebrow comically.

"Tee-hee," I laughed feebly. Parents can really say some depressing crap at night when they're tired.

He flipped to another page in the album. "Here it is. All the fun I was having."

I put my head down real close and brought the page up, too. Sure enough, he seemed to actually be having fun, though it was hard to be certain.

"Man, Arizona was wild back then," my old man claimed. "The Beehive Club, whoopee! Whadda joint. Able Cactus Dance Pavilion. Great dames. Some hot cats, too. Yeah!"

Then he flipped to another page and swung it around to showing me more of what he had talked about, all the fun he was having in the swing band and what it had been like when he was with the guys playing big band music in the forties. Saguaro cactuses. Dames. And big brass trombones.

"You're dressed as a clown," I pointed out with the bravery and damned brain power God grants twelve-year-olds.

"Yes, we...ah...performed as clowns," he said happily. My old man actually wasn't embarrassed about the fact that he'd dressed himself up as a clown. In extra-large photos, my old man, I hate to say it, was wearing a baggy white silk costume and a big nose, probably red (as I said, the photos were black and white back then). They even stuck these dunce caps on their heads, doing the clown thing to the tee, and having crazy enormous pom-poms like cabbages sewn down the front of their costumes. Cabbage, cabbage, cabbage. This was part of the ridiculous junk he wanted me to share in.

The old man didn't notice, or preferred to pretend not to notice, my horror at the idea that he had performed in this absurd costume. I mean, damn, a boy wants his Dad to have some dignity. You know the kids of the knights of old in England got to be pages and followed their fathers into battle in armor and good-looking metal chainmail, so they say in *Ivanhoe*. And he was showing himself to me in a silky clown's costume!

"This was my best friend, Chauncey," said Dad, tapping the photo of another band member sitting near him.

"He was a clown, too," I pointed out.

Dad turned quickly to another page of the album. The old man took no notice of my growing depression. "My 1935 Ford. Mom drove me up to the used car lot to pay for it. $350 smackers. Man that was the slickest car. When I finished working on it."

A real gas, or a ball, that was what he'd had. According to my old man. A real gas with those band guys and that car. Wild clubs and bars were his hangouts, and he drove around the desert, and on the back roads of mountains, in the fast Ford, which he bought with the savings from playing in bands, and he bragged about getting lots of girls, or so he told me, though he might have been bullshitting, you know, I was only twelve at the time and couldn't tell too well when a grown-up man was bullshitting. This band idea sounded pretty good to me from behind my thick glasses.

"I've an idea... James. For you to have...for me to let you have...my trombone. My idea is that you would borrow it for a while. If, as I think, you'll agree, you want to take band in junior high."

The actual point was gotten to. My engineering father took forever to build up a premise, to build the foundations of a simple goddamned question. And the old man's question was: would I want to play the trombone like he had?

"Sure, I guess so. Why not? Would it get me outta P.E.?" I asked hopefully. P.E. was a bad scene for me. You see my eyesight is terrible and I'm always tripping over things. Sometimes I fall over my own feet.

"No. I don't think it will replace P.E.," he answered, honestly enough.

"Um. Okay."

"It might get you out of chorus, though," he offered.

"Oh, that would be pretty good. My voice is the pits."

"I understand," said my old man.

Using a blue cartridge pen, I filled out the card, Arizona Public School, District One, Elective Request, printing "7th grade band" in the indicated space. After school: Model Rocketry Club or Vietnam War Combat Club.

What a jerk I was then about that Vietnam club. Combat Club, jeez. I didn't even like P.E. and now I'm bummed out all day about what I have to do to get out of the damn Vietnam draft. Seven more months and I'm eighteen. Have to register thirty days before my birthday. But Nixon isn't calling up anyone born in 1955—yet.

CHAPTER TWO

At the beginning of every band class the junior high band instructor, Mr. Gomez, would stand at the door greeting students—"Hey, Petey. *Hola*, Josue. Hi, Robert."

And my greeting?

He tapped me on the head with a handy baton or a pencil and said, "Jaime. Exactly like my little brother Alfred."

Mr. Gomez hated me. Because I reminded him of his little brother, who must have been a royal pain in the ass, a real horror, given the way he decided to send bad vibes at me for two long years.

It used to make my face and my neck and my ears turn bright red. I know this because the guys in the trombone section would yak at me about it non-stop.

"James, your face is bright red!"

"James, your ears are really red!"

"Even your neck is red, man!"

"Jaime, is there any part of you that isn't red, man?"

Guys in band then took to calling me Little Alfred the Asshole, though my name is James, not Alfred, I'm not really short or anything, and I happen not to be an asshole, thank you very much for zilch.

"Little Alfred!"

"Take this, Alfred!"

"Hey Alfred, you're a real dick!"

Uncool cats who wouldn't let up on me began whacking me over the head with pencils or anything they had handy every goddamned time they saw me in the halls or the cafeteria. Lunch bags with apple cores in them rained down on me. Rolled up tests bopped my poor little bruised brain. Forks even thumped me. I was bugged by a bunch of jerks for no reason other than what this band teacher had said. This alone should have made me hate band, right? But I didn't. I liked the old Souza garbage.

Then there were these two infuriating finks in Model Rocketry Club who took the old Let's Torture James Thing to an extreme and used to bash me over the head with my model rocket and call out sarcastically for everyone to hear: "I launch you, Alfred the Asshole" like I was a ship or something and they were christening me with a bottle. If they'd had a real heavy glass bottle, a Coke or something, they probably would have smashed me over the head with it and killed me, the damn jerks. Their model rockets were badly built, even worse than mine. And no, I didn't take Vietnam Combat Club. Ever.

Let me tell you, riding your bike with a banana seat for a couple of miles with a trombone case banging your knees is the pits. Shoot man, holding onto the case handle and the bike handle was tricky. I used to try to set the case on my left knee, crosswise, you see, and let the weight of the trombone go up and down while I rode one-handed. The bell part of the case would whack my elbow a lot, though, which was really annoying. I kept trying to figure out ways to strap the trombone onto the banana seat. I didn't have one of those cool stingray bikes that were smaller and were made to go with the banana seat. No, I had the banana seat stuck onto a regular-sized bike, because you could buy the banana seat as an add-on and that was the cheap-o way my parents thought I would experience a stingray bike. Anyway, on windy March days in the desert a big old trombone case crosswise creates a sort of extra wing off the side of my regular-sized bike with the banana seat and the wind wanted to rip the trombone out of my hand or knock the bike and me over. The way to think of it is that the bike and trombone became a kite which is pretty hard to correct for, and I crashed a couple of times into shrubs and signs, but no cactus patches, luckily, although I had few close calls. And I didn't damage my old man's trombone. I usually got a ride in the car to school if it was windy and rainy, thank goodness, but rain's pretty much a zilch in the desert. You can't count on that coming. Or if you do, you're stupid. And riding your bike was even less fun when it's like ninety going on a hundred degrees in May and early June and your home is two miles away across scalding hot pavement and dusty, empty desert lots. My parents consider that normal everyday conditions and did not give me, or my sisters, rides home from school for the prospect of extreme scorching, f-ing heat at three-thirty every damn afternoon. Trombone or no trombone they expected me to ride home through my personal version of hell. But hells on earth have a way of changing. That one of mine came to an end as high school approached.

◆ ◆ ◆

"Being in band in high school is going to brand you as hopelessly uncool, James. You do know that, don't you?" my older sister Gertrude explained during one of her visits on a blazing hot Sunday at the end of junior high.

As a judge of what was cool and uncool, I was beginning to trust Gertrude completely. She had managed to get herself together and escape from her life as a jerk wearing dorky clothes and working at the public library a few years earlier. Now she worked at the Anthropology Department at the University and she talked about cool things like Margaret Mead's theories and sex as it was practiced in jungle groups. And she no longer lived in Parental Weirdsville, U.S.A. More power to her.

"I don't think Mom and Dad will let me drop out," I said. "Besides, Dad said I might be in a band and have some wild times, getting into nightclubs and stuff." Behind my thick glasses, I know my eyes must have looked crazy, searching her face for help.

"Uh-uh. So you're actually gonna take his word for it? You

aren't gonna have any wild times in a band, kid-o. Band is totally uncool. What rock bands use trombones? They only want guitars. And the drinking age is dropping to 19. You might be able to sneak into bars on your own without being in a band. And I promise as soon as I'm in an apartment for a few more months you can come over and spend a night and we'll smoke marijuana if you have a day off. Christmas or Rodeo, maybe. If I can."

Big deal. Christmas or Rodeo were pretty far off, so this wasn't much of a gift. I sure was a desperate jerk, because I think I said: "Hey, thanks. You're probably right. Band in high school is really dumb. I want to drop out of band so badly." I did realize the truth of what she was saying. Shoot, why bother joining a band when you could sneak into a bar real easily or get marijuana?

"Do it then, James. Just do it."

"I've got the itch now. The itch to be free! Also, I'm not walking across the desert and down through an arroyo to our high school with a goddamned lead-ass trombone case hanging at my side every day. A few guys have it in for me, and they're planning to make my life miserable in high school, and they might be smoking marijuana in the arroyo. If they were to see me coming along, they would be sure to jump me and beat me up, if they hadn't started smoking yet, that is."

"Right on. You won't be able to out run them, or even get out of the arroyo very fast with a damned trombone weighing you down and you being blind."

"Yup. Well, blind-ish. I can see, sorta."

"They might even wreck Dad's trombone and then you'd really be in trouble."

"Oh yeah, crud. And Mom and Dad think I'm part of the in crowd. They believe I couldn't possibly have an enemy in the world. If Dad's trombone gets damaged they'll think I deliberately damaged it. They live in cuckoo land, no matter what I try to tell them about what really is happening at school and how crammed full of jerks the world is."

"That's an old story," my older sister said in her best, worn-out older sister voice. "They aren't gonna listen to that."

My plan after this talk with my sister was to drop band as an elective and put art or drama in its place. I liked those subjects and both of those classes had a lot cuter girls in them, too. This I had been told by Gertrude.

My attempt to convince my parents of my desire to be out of band, however, did not succeed.

Something else came in as an important ridiculous factor to make me fill out my high school preference card with band as an elective. My mother is what that was.

◆ ◆ ◆

"You know, James, your father and I have never been lucky enough to appear on television," Mother said, like a holy martyr or something one afternoon when she was ironing my white T shirts. She thought I ought to wear ironed white T-shirts under my buttoned-down shirt. White T-shirts under buttoned-down shirts was not really the style anymore, even in Arizona, and I'd been trying unsuccessfully to tell her that nobody had white T shirts under their shirts and it was also a hot late spring when it was already one hundred degrees, and riding a bike home with two shirts on would be suicide, but she wouldn't listen. She kept on ironing shirts and yakking about her dumb wish that I would appear on TV.

I should explain that she is a total television nut. I mean she watches anything that is on the boob tube. And she worshipped the stars. She had our house built so a little TV den was on the other side of the kitchen, with only a low wall separating them, and she could hear the TV and stand on tip-toes at the stove and see the picture while she was cooking! Dad, as I said, had his own TV in the converted carport den.

Anyway, my appearing on TV wasn't a matter of vanity or anything like that. She didn't think I was so damn handsome or charming, though she doesn't hate me or anything, I guess. No, the reason she wanted me on TV was a matter of family equality.

"Both your sisters," she went on, "got to be on The Deputy JGUN Hour of Fun when they were little. I want you to have the same opportunity."

This Deputy JGUN jerk was a skinny ding-a-ling who was famous locally a few years ago for inviting birthday boys and girls to his studio and sitting them on bleachers and then lining them up while he sat in a chair and spanked them over his lap on their butts right on live TV! Hell, the whole thing was pretty sick-o and he combined it with cartoons and goofy skits about the Wild West and stuff. Both my sisters, Gertrude and Ginny, got to do that, to go down to the studio and line up with the birthday kids for Deputy JGUN, with their undies and slip showing and all, but for some reason or other it never worked out that I got to go to the Deputy JGUN Show on my birthday which was a little too close to Christmas, I guess. But shoot, my mother in her brain of motherly justice, fairness and equality had cooked up, slowly and painfully, the way only a real sick-o mother could, this really weird but deeply felt nuts-o idea that I had somehow been shortchanged in the television appearance department, and that I was only hiding my deep disappointment with the fact that I hadn't been on TV.

"You ought to appear on television at **some** time in your life," Mom said, narrowing her eyes at me. "If you're in the band, you're going to march in the Rodeo parade. And that's a sure-fire way to get on TV. In the Rodeo Parade you can see everybody and with a trombone you're gonna be in front!" She was right in part because the high school bands all marched in the annual rodeo parade in town, and the parade was always filmed and shown once live and once again that night. There was a good chance that your band member would walk right by the camera sometime during the parade.

I saw that she was planning to make a big deal out of this. "I don't like television," I explained. "And," connecting my ideas, "I don't want to join the band in order to be on the thing that I hate, see?"

"You don't like TV because you never sit still and watch a whole show."

"The idiocy drives me away."

"What?"

"It's dumb. Television is dumb."

"It isn't."

"I'll challenge you!" I cried. I wanted to be bold about my opinions. I'd been working on that.

"What?"

"I will watch all of one of your favorite shows once to prove to you that I don't like it!"

"Okay."

"What's your favorite show? Pick one!" I said.

"*The Merv Griffin Show*, but I like tons of others."

"Just one. One. Yeah, I should have known that practically anything on TV is your favorite show, but you have to pick one. So, *Merv Griffin* it is."

The next day, after I watched *The Merv Griffin Show* with her, I had to say I didn't know why she liked that show.

"That was about the dumbest show besides *Sea Hunt*, *Love, American Style* and *The Family Affair Show* and there's really some dumb stuff on," I told her at the end of the show when they went to the sponsor messages.

"All right, Mr. Smarty-Pants. I guess you're entitled to your opinion, but don't persecute me with it."

"Who's that jerky English guy on the sofa?"

"That jerky English guy, as you call him, is a well-known London celebrity—" and she said some name like Percival Marleybones, or something. Maybe I ought to have told my old man that she had a thing for that dumb jerk Mervin and some phony Marleybones that's sitting around with him talking to his guests like they're in somebody's living room.

"You never were cocky like this before," Mother gasped. "This is exactly what happens when someone feels deprived. Now I know you've got to get on television."

"Mom, listen, I do not need to be on television. What I need is to get some new Levis. I have to have bellbottoms when I go to high school. Everybody's wearing them and I don't want to be left out anymore. I want to fit in."

"What difference does the bottom of the pant make? You have pants, don't you?"

"These aren't stylish anymore."

"If everybody jumped off a cliff, would you follow them?" Mom asked in a sing-song voice that drove me crazy. This is the stupidest question ever invented by a parent.

"Am I wearing straight-legged pants at the edge of this cliff? Because then I might!"

Put a long disappointed pause in there.

And then a crazy response.

Since I showed anger over the state of my Levi's, she decided that I was still brooding over the fact that I hadn't been on TV!

"I think your problem, young man," she said, "is that you're disappointed. I knew I should have gotten you on TV once. It makes all the difference. The girls perked up right away when they went on TV."

"They were six years old! Six-year-olds perk up all the time! What I'm brooding over, Mom, is the state of my wardrobe. I need better Levi's and when are you going to let me buy some bitchin' looking bellbottoms and a Nehru shirt instead of the straight-legs and tight button down shirts that are turning me into a creep?"

"You know I don't like that word—'bitchin.' Your father told you to stop using it. I can see you're hiding your deep disappointment about not being on TV," she said.

There it was again. Dang, she had a one-track mind. And the sure-fire way that I could appear on television was to join a high school band. What screwy thinking. Who in the heck besides my mother cared about being on TV? It was as though she thought I wasn't going to be a real person if I'd never appeared on television or something.

"Plato and Socrates weren't on TV. Genghis Khan wasn't interviewed on TV. Both of them survived until they died.

They never suffered without an appearance on TV!" I observed. Perhaps you've noticed that I was coming unglued at that point.

"I've decided!" she exclaimed. "You have to join the high school band or be mixed up for life!"

Hell, it was crazy the way she went on yakking about that TV appearance.

"Mom, the only thing I feel deprived about is not being able to get a pair of bellbottoms and get rid of my dorky, straight-legged pants."

"Your cousins in Indiana would be glad to have pants as nice as the straight-legged ones I bought you. They're grateful children."

"Okay, Mom," I said furiously, "here's what you do. Get a box. Cram it full with these straight-legged pants that I hate. Send that goddamned box off to my cousins in Indiana cause they don't know the difference between what's stylish and what isn't, and let me buy myself some bellbottoms and a Nehru styled shirt!"

I saw it coming. Sorta.

She slapped me.

That was a snide comment about her relatives, who, lord knows, honestly, did not care what was popular to wear, but pointing out the truth was something which Mother deeply resented. It was a nasty crack about her relatives. Ladies get sensitive about nasty cracks about their nephews who spend most of their time in canoes jerking off along the goddamned muddy Salamone River.

So, she got so mad at me about that bellbottom crack that she slapped my impudent face and said she would tell my Dad and get me punished if I didn't agree to join high school band. So, of course, I joined the damn band. It was a bummer. My plan of getting out of Band Squaresville in high school was shot-down. Well, I really didn't have anything against bands, or marching, or the trombone. In fact I sort of thought it was fun to be in the band. Man, things got complicated after that, though. One thing led to another, and two springs later I ended up spending a lot of my Saturdays and Sundays playing in a Shriner Band. Yeah. For real. Shriners.

CHAPTER THREE

As I now slide my trombone under my bed for good, sliding it into the sunset so to speak and saying *adios*, *amigo*, *hasta la vista*, and so forth, as I have faithfully not learned in Spanish from *Sr.* O' Shaunnesey in fourth period, I can confidently proclaim to you today that a trombone is a really bitchin' instrument for two reasons that I know. These reasons I've learned over the time I was taking lessons with Gluey and playing for the Shriners.

One reason trombones are great is they're a vocal instrument—that was the way to describe the trombone—according to the spiel, a grumbling, mumbling spiel I suffered through when I met Mr. Frank K. McGluen, on my first day of lessons. Think of the world as made up of band instruments. Some instruments—like clarinets—they squeal at you all the time. And others are like the bulging tubas: too heavy and they blow kinda dull and dark. Some instruments like flutes are too sweet for their own good. Now it takes all types to make beautiful music in this world; I know this. I can talk extemporaneously, bullshitting out loud really, for a long time about band instruments and people, if you have the time to sit down and listen to me. And what I would tell you was the real honest-to-goodness truth, which is that trombones can talk in a lot of voices. Like a person.

And the other thing I learned is fairly simple and that is that besides percussion, the trombone section is one of the only sections in any band that can laugh while they're playing. I didn't just memorize that from the first lecture Mr. McGluen gave me in his pathetic little living room. I actually learned a lot about life and laughing from playing the trombone for Gluey.

Oh, and another thing is if you have a trombone you can open your spit valve on your annoying little sister.

Spit valves. I haven't said anything about those.

A spit valve is a really nifty thing on a trombone and it's located on the bottom of the slide. When you play the trombone, spit builds up inside the instrument as you play, sorta condensing out of your breath. If you don't do anything about this condensation, you will hear the notes bubbling and gurgling through a damn ocean of your own sputum eventually. It's pretty funny and gross. You can keep on playing and make this interesting gurgling noise. Very grody so far, right? That is the point at which you need to open the spit valve and watch your warm oozy spit come dripping out, splat, splat, and splat. What a blast! That part's bitchin', amazingly so. I also liked to chase my little sister Ginny around the house with the trombone in my hands when my mom isn't home, threatening to open the spit valve on her. The first time I opened it on Ginny's neck from behind and she howled for a long time and took a shower, something she hates to do because she's heard about this movie where a lady gets stabbed to death in the shower. It was a goddamned blast listening to her complain. Heavenly.

Talking about spit valves and other grody things, for your education, I knew a kid in my junior high band who liked to play trombone with candy in his mouth. Every day he brought in a different candy which he ate, and Mr. Gomez never caught him eating the stuff when he was playing because he was so sneaky about it. The kid thought he was really cool. But over time the little bits of candy that he chewed blew out of his mouth and that candy built up in his spit in the trombone slide. Until one day.

Blowing and blowing, playing some song we were going to perform for the spring concert, but not a peep or a bleat was coming from that horn, man. He kept on blowing all the same. Man, he was an optimist, I guess. Just imagine this bright red face of this kid struggling away as he tried to get some air to go through his trombone, but he couldn't make a pathetic little toot come out. Finally, Mr. Gomez noticed what was happening and he came charging over like the invasion of Normandy or the goddamned charge up San Juan Hill or something like that.

"We need to clean that instrument," he said angrily, smashing his way through the folding chairs and instrument cases toward the red-faced trombonist.

"Okay, okay," said the kid, yanking the slide out before Mr. Gomez got to him.

"Where's your cleaning tool?" Mr. Gomez demanded when he reached the candy kid.

"I haven't got one of those," the boy said, handing over his slide.

"Well, borrow one, now!" thundered Mr. Gomez.

I fumbled around for mine, being a goddamned Good Samaritan (too much Congregational church, I suppose) and all that, but a boy who was nearer gave up his cleaning tool.

Mr. Gomez snatched the slide away from the boy and held it up. He looked in the slide hole. "I can see a blockage!" he yelled. "There is definitely a blockage in this instrument!"

Most band teachers go ape over blockages. They all have hang-ups about gunk in valuable instruments.

Then he stuck the cleaning snake in the trombone slide. All the time he was grumbling and growling. Of course, he couldn't get the snake to move through at the point at the bottom of the slide where the spit valve was. He pushed and pushed and even cursed, mildly in Spanish, the old carumba and Chihuahua deal, because he was actually surrounded by junior high school students. Finally when he got whatever it was all the way around, and it came out the end, what squirted out was a plug of candy spit that was all the colors of the rainbow, or all the colors of the candies, the boy had sucked. The plug was a real pastel nightmare, which was very interesting. I was close enough to see the disgusting thing because I was in the trombone section, but a higher chair than that boob. It was fascinating to look at what came out, sorta like the rocks in the Grand Canyon or something, as it lay in the band leader's trash can. Striated, that's the word, and he let all his students take a long look at this striated gunk as we left the band room so that he could make a big deal out of how a stupid jerk like that guy could really ruin a perfectly good instrument by playing while chewing candy. After that, the kid's job was to clean instruments for a whole month and his parents had to pick him up at 4:30 instead of 3:30 and ball him out a whole bunch over and over again. I don't know if he was spanked by the Vice Principal or not, but they were still doing that when I was in junior high. I hear they quit that last year.

◆ ◆ ◆

Junior high school had only just ended, I had finished my eighth grade year, when I began private trombone lessons with Frank McGluen. The reason I took private lessons was I couldn't get in the high school band unless I showed that I had taken some outside private lessons. You see how the ramifications of this thing are expanding like the plot of a goddamned Russian novel or something? But did I want to be in the goddamned high school band? Hell no! As I said, my father and mother were the ones who wanted me to be in the band so that I could march in the rodeo parade and they could see me on TV. Talk about a jerky chain of reasoning.

"Have a lot of fun," said Ginny, in an especially snotty voice when I opened the back door of our car and got out with my trombone. "This is gonna be super neat-o." She has always excelled at making a person feel like crap.

"Oh, flake off, will you?" I replied. "Do you have to bug me non-stop?"

"Yes. I do. Bye, bye." She waved this uncool little finky wave of hers. Despicable.

My mom and Ginny didn't pull away from the curb in that grand old chariot of ours, the white 1967 Plymouth Belvedere, even after I had opened the little gate in the chain link fence and walked with my trombone case in hand up to the tiny yellow brick house with the skuzzy front door to my first lesson with Gluey. "Why don't you go?" I called back to them in the car.

"Go on up to the door," Mom hollered.

Ginny, the little dip-shit, fell over laughing.

"Yes, look at me! I am doing that," I said sarcastically.

I guessed from the worried way Mom was looking at me that she was waiting to see if the ax murderer was going to run out of that cruddy little house and stab me in the forehead with an ice pick or I mean an ax or something. An ax murderer would chose to live in an unassuming homey but junky little place like that house Gluey was in. And I'm pretty sure my little sister had some high hopes along the lines of ax murderers and my forehead. Often it was plain from the look on her face that she relished me getting into problems and troubles. Most of the time she was rooting for my failure and would add to my problems, though I must admit that I really liked it when she got into big trouble at school for throwing Bermuda grass around in the faces of kids on the playground. She had thought the teacher was not looking out the window or couldn't see that far back. Ha! I coulda told her he had a pair of binoculars.

Anyway, that day when I was going to my first private trombone lesson, I gave them a really angry wave-off signal, like leave me alone you dorks, which Mother ignored. She had spooky dark glasses on and was staring at me, leaning forward past my sister, I suppose she was leaning like that so she could see Mr. McGluen when I went into the house. She hadn't met him and had taken the high school band director's recommendation of Mr. McGluen sight unseen, though I know she talked to him on the phone. Well, if she was so damned worried I don't know why she didn't just hold my hand while we walked up to the door. Or why the hell didn't she sit in the same room knitting or something while I took the first lesson.

I stood on the concrete walkway looking at the plain dirt front yard of the house. Packed dirt. Fuzzy weeds crawling with bumps that looked like beetles along a fence where no one could get at them. Some girl's abandoned tricycle waiting in the dirt. Honestly, my vision, even with my glasses, isn't that perfect, so I couldn't see much more.

I moved forward all the while fuming at my mother and sister for being so annoying, and then I found myself stomping up the two red concrete steps to the door and jabbing the lighted doorbell.

Jack shit, that's what happened next. There was me, not groovy, standing in front of Gluey's lousy house with the splintery front door. Note please that I did not think this crappy door was an auspicious beginning to our relationship. I like that word, auspicious, and I have been trying to stick it into auspicious places whenever and wherever I find them. Vocab word courtesy junior year High School English,.

There were these three enormous eucalyptus trees on the west side of his home and the porch at his door was in the shade of one of them and was so cool even in the first week of June in Arizona when I first showed up at his door. After a minute or two, I rang the doorbell again, and I remember I was kinda enjoying standing there, imagining this was my first crappy house and I lived in it alone, having friends, especially girlfriends, over for crazy parties, smoking dope, listening to something besides Tijuana Brass on my own stereo. Then two things happened.

First, Mr. McGluen opened the door. "Hello, James, is it?"

Second, the splinters along the bottom of the door snagged the green wool carpet, so that he couldn't even pull it back cleanly, which was ridiculous. "Dear, dear, this door got warped in the last monsoon. Need a new one!" he exclaimed.

Third, I got my first look at him. My initial impression was that Frank McGluen looked like a large, unpleasant white grub or a huge blob of wet Elmer's glue, and that, of course, explained his nickname of Gluey, which was everybody's name for him at my high school.

Gluey had blonde hair, shaved in a crew cut, and wiry

blonde eyebrows above dark eyes that always looked intense and motivated like someone who wanted to tell you a story about a boss adventure he'd had. He was short and pudgy and, of course, very pale. He liked to wear suede shoes and polyester slacks that were a little too short. When he was seated, the pant legs rode up and there was always a gap between his sock and his pants where you could see how white his sickly skin was. The Elmer Glue skin of his. He wore belts in his pants and golfing shirts, but I don't think he ever golfed. His arms were hairless. Sometimes he wore one of those bola ties with a hunk of a shimmery golden red rock with his golfing shirt, and that kind of bola tie was popular among real uncool people. A bola tie in a golf shirt was weird looking, even weird for actual weird people.

I looked at Gluey for the first time in my life and then I heard the car with my mother and sister in it pulling away from the curb. I swung around and glared as my sister stuck her tongue out at me because she knew how miserable I felt. I didn't want to go to private trombone lessons. Certainly not in the first month of summer right before I was heading to high school. So there I was at four o'clock in the afternoon on the first summer Monday about to take private lessons with a weird white grub. Depressing? You have no idea. I'd planned to memorize some lyrics off of album covers and get Gertrude to teach me to dance The Jerk and the Booga-loo before high school. I had not gone to any of my junior high dances and I vowed to attend the ones in high school, but I needed to dance better, not to mention getting my act together. Gertrude owned a '61 Beetle and I was gonna learn some things about driving from her and look over engine parts so when I got my first car I could take care of it. I had a friend named Scott and he and I were planning to hike in the mountains to this cool canyon camp full of cool hip people that we'd heard about. These private trombone lessons were sorta interfering with my mental preparation to get it together and achieve coolness in high school.

Gluey had gotten the inside track to my high school's music lesson business because he and my band director went to Juilliard together. I think he was from Pennsylvania or New Jersey originally. I have to say he was a very fine musician. All the mothers at high school thought that their little angels would study with this great guy and end up going to Juilliard under his tutelage. What I have to say about that is "yeah, right suckers, fat chance given that you're from the backward state of Arizona, a state which has a skinny jackass of a one-eyed governor named Happy Jack who hates anything intellectual and the state has no culture at all, anyway, unless you're interested in Navajo rugs or Hopi pots or identifying the crop insects that are dangerous to cotton, oranges, dates and alfalfa." And our state assets? Cotton, copper, climate and commerce. Arizona, to a c. What a crock of crap!

The house where Gluey lived was made of regular red bricks, not adobe, but they'd been painted yellow probably twenty years earlier and never repainted again. The sun had really done a number on them and the fascia and about every inch of the house was peeling or buckling. Really, I'd have to say there were so many paint chips around the side of his property that it looked like the color was flowing away across the damned desert, and so much buckling paint that it looked like the poor house had eczema. It was an incredibly teeny home as teeny desert houses go, and they do make them small here to save on materials. After all, it's pretty nice outside for most of the fall, winter and spring, so why do you even need a house? You could live in your backyard, BBQ, eat on a picnic bench, and sleep on a cot under a tree. But I mean I live in a smallish brick house, okay, though I guess it was a custom home, but this thing Gluey lived in was the kind of house a young Air Force guy would stay in all by himself listening to some dumb piece of music, or maybe something good like Iron Butterfly's "In a Gadda Da Vida" over and over again, and I picked that because we had that playing at our church confirmation dance, over and over and over, and this Air Force guy would be studying the album cover, and burning a fat orange candle that smelled like furniture wax. Who'da thought a guy who graduated from Juilliard and stuff would live in an itsy bitsy dump of a house like that one out in the desert? With crap evaporative cooling—a swamp box we call it— instead of air conditioning. Shouldn't he have been someone big in New York or something? Shouldn't he be in some orchestra somewhere? That was the first thing that struck me. Not that I cared or anything, because as far as I'm concerned it's live and let live, but it was an interesting observation. Why in the world was he living like this? Obviously, he was a big failure at life. There was no other conclusion you could draw, I told myself. And he had a kid, too. That was the middle class values of me coming out thinking a house had to be all fake magnificent and everything. I thought adults were supposed to pretend, at least, to be successful. I defined success in a very conventional manner, probably because my parents valued middle class objects over having any kind of higher calling. They wouldn't have understood the concept of a higher calling if it was going to cost them any actual comfort.

"Put your trombone case next to the chair," Gluey said.

"Okay, sir." I set my trombone case beside one of the two dinged-up metal folding chairs in the middle of a sad living room.

I sat down.

"No, no, I want to show you some of my instruments and funny things." He urged me to get up and walk around the room.

The furniture was old dingy stuff like my parents had in photos of when they first married. Dinky sofas with mustard-colored fabric. Scratchier than hell because it was the type of fabric that bumped up like caterpillars. Thick planks of blonde wood for table and sofa legs. He had musical instruments mounted on the walls, mostly trombones. Around the trombones he had these horrible clown and circus poodle paintings that looked to have been paint-by-numbers. (I know about paint-by-numbers because Ginny loves those sets and has begged me to admire her work on them many times). These creepy paintings were in frames made out of cholla cactus, the type of cactus wood that is full of holes, and that was super strange. His walls were painted moss green. Moss green walls! Heck that was really old fashioned. And I remember his living room lamp was one of those miniature chuck wagons made out of cholla cactus that you bought as a kit and made yourself. Real crazy jip-o stuff.

I noticed the stacks and stacks of LPs and 78s that he kept on shelves and in overflowing piles. A very new stereo was about the only modern thing he had in the whole place. He obviously loved his music.

Gluey led me around his dinky living room and a hall, too, and went on and on about the different trombones he owned and what each one meant to him. About his trombones and his slides and all, Gluey was a real nut. I don't remember much of what he showed me, but Gluey owned a huge number of interesting instruments, silver trombones and special old trombones and lots of slides. I guess I remember him showing me a funny run-over slide he had, and one he'd painted black for some reason like he'd thought it would look cool that way when he was young, but just about when I finally thought he was going to lecture me about the Austrians putting trombones in their music and the great pieces composed for trombones, he did something I never would have thought of. He got around to the essence of what he thought made the trombone special.

"There're many special things about a trombone, James. One of the things is that it used to be called the sackbut. That is one funny name for an instrument. Anything with the word butt in it is probably good, huh?"

"I guess so, sir," I said stiffly. I was being a jerk about lessons still.

"Another special thing about a trombone," he continued as we took our seats on the beat-up folding chairs, "is that more than any other instrument in all the orchestra a trombone is able to sound like a human voice." He played something so I could hear that. He was good at it and made his trombone talk, and cry, and whine, and weep, and sing. He even made it cough. "But the really special thing about a trombone is that you can laugh

while you're playing. Let me show you how and you can start practicing laughing while playing right away."

"What, sir?" I said, interrupting him immediately as I came awake. His deep voice had kinda lulled me to sleep. I was sure he hadn't said "laugh". I was mad at myself for daydreaming like that. "Ah, sir, did you just say you want me to practice laughing while playing?" Hearing him wrong seemed the only possibility. No one could have said anything as ridiculous as that.

"That's right," he said patiently, as though he thought I were a real dumbo or something, "I want to show you how to laugh while you're playing so that it doesn't change your tone materially. It's an important skill in any band. Indispensable, really, in many situations. Things that happen around musicians are crazy at times."

Man, I couldn't believe it. Who was he kidding? It was absurd! But I was proud of myself because I was able to control my reaction and I didn't snort or anything, though I really wanted to. I mean really, at that point I thought, gee, this guy is a crazy kook or something. "Don't you want to criticize my embouchure, and tell me my vacuum over the mouthpiece isn't perfect or my upper lip isn't going over my lower the right way or something?" I asked.

"No, I don't think I'll talk about that too much. I took the liberty of phoning your junior high band director, Rogelio Gomez, and he said you were a pretty good player with good technique and you could read music. But just to be sure, if you want me to, I can check. Show me your embouchure."

I showed him my embouchure, without my instrument, which, by the way, is the way I held my mouth when I played the trombone. I'd been told I had a pretty good one and I wanted him to say that again because I was looking for a little positive feedback, so to speak.

"Well, that looks fine. Now listen to me play."

Then he played for me–he was really good, amazing actually, playing some big band crap—and then he laughed out of the side of his mouth. He snuck it in in a strange way, and I'll be damned, he didn't miss a note and the music didn't change one bit, but he was laughing real good, a boss belly laugh.

Then he made me get out my trombone and he watched me put it together and he had me oil the slide and play the same music and try to mimic him, playing along and laughing. He tapped the music where he had written the word "laugh" and I was supposed to try laughing then, but it was the pits. The music fell apart until there was basically nothing coming out of my horn. It was going to take a lot of practice to get any good at laughing and playing music any time soon.

"Work on that," he said quietly, "give it some of your time and effort. I can't offer you much of a hint about how to do it. You'll have to develop your own technique. But I can tell you it comes in handy. There's always something funny going on with a bunch of musicians together. I've had to use my laughing technique lots of times myself and it's been a critical skill. Critical, James. For parades, especially. I have a lesson notebook for you here and I want you to bring it with you every time you come. Do you understand?"

"Yeah, sure."

"I'm going to write that laughing practice in right now. 'Ten minutes of practice laughing while playing any music you like.' You write 'laugh' in on the measure you want and try to continue playing and laughing." And I swear he actually wrote that in on the first line of my lesson notebook. I still have it, so I can remember he actually assigned that and I wasn't imagining it. Nobody will ever believe me, probably.

"So, you want me to call you James, James?" said Gluey, talking quietly. "That's the way you want me to address you?"

"Yes, sir. I don't like Jim, or Jimmie. I really hate Jimmie, sir. If you don't mind me saying it, being called Jimmie makes me want to puke."

"Jimmie would be an insult. That's what they call a diminutive of the name James. You call a bawling five-year-old boy Jimmie. Not a teenager. I'm going to put your name down in my book as James and put a record of your mother's payment in there."

That's the way he told me to get out the payment. He was subtle about money, real suave-like. I had the bills my mother had given me crammed in my front pocket. Three smackers. He wrote out a receipt with a goofy lady's pen which he kept in a teeny plastic box with fake jewels on it. He always kept that itsy-bitsy pen in its box on his music stand. It was the kind of thing a lady got in her Christmas stocking. A Canasta prize or something. I'll bet his wife lent him that screwy thing as a big joke. As I said, I needed the receipt from him in order to prove I had taken private lessons before they'd let me into band at high school.

The next week I came back with my music, which was the "Swing Time March" by Souza, with "laugh" written in on a measure and with me trying to put real laughing in at the point where I'd noted that I would. I'd tried screwing my mouth up different ways in order to laugh while playing and while I had been able to make notes come out, they weren't really up to snuff yet, and I knew it. Gluey listened gravely while I played the piece and I tried to laugh on the measure where I'd written it. I was too uptight, though. The music crashed, although I had practiced several times that week exactly as he'd suggested. I was bummed.

After I'd finished, he nodded and lied, saying that I was "beginning to succeed at playing and laughing." That was definitely not true. I was terrible at it and had destroyed the piece.

"Do about the same amount of time practicing laughing again this week, James. Don't forget to do it, but don't get stressed out about it. If you worry too much, you won't be able to play and laugh. Your laughing has to be easy-going." Gluey didn't seem in the least discouraged by my failure as he wrote in my lesson book. Also, he didn't smile while assigning me to laugh while playing, but acted like it was something important and serious.

What happened next was way-out, man. His white hand reached over to a pile of sheet music. That pile held all his music that he was assigning for pupils. He grabbed the top sheet.

Wham. Right on the stand in front of me. The first piece of music from him. Oh, man, it was weird.

"This first assignment is a duet, James," said Gluey.

Man, I have to tell you I was freaked out by what he had picked for me. In a world full of great music, he had chosen to give me some damn nutty circus music.

A screamer, they call them. I knew right away what it was. The composer was Karl King. He wrote hundreds of those damn screamers to excite people in circuses. My band director told us about them in junior high and we played a simple one once. I wondered what was going on with this guy for him to have picked this piece of music. It was crazy.

I took a second look. Yeah, that was right, it was the type of music that was used to get the circus audience excited and their attention riveted on the big lion act or the clowns or the entry of the bear on the motorcycle or some death-defying stunt on the trapeze or high wire. I thought he was going to give me high-brow stuff like they would play at Juilliard, a classical duet, something written by a major composer at least on a serious theme, the death of some classical god or a battle or an ode to spring or a dying fawn. I thought he was grooming me for the symphony business. Highbrow crap and all that. Well, you'd think that from someone who went to Juilliard for heaven sake, wouldn't you? But instead he was giving me this circus crap. It was real nuts!

"This is a screamer," I said to him bluntly after I had glanced at the title and the composer one last time.

Gluey cleared his throat, I suppose in order to delay answering me, and because I had caught him at something he hadn't been prepared for. "You are fundamentally correct, James. They do call this a screamer."

"I didn't expect you to give me something like this," I told him.

"Ah, well. The screamer, James, is a highly esteemed music in my opinion, a very demanding type of music due to the rapid and advanced rhythms they use, especially the low-brass parts. Trombone and tuba. Good stuff." He added this goofy defense in an attempt to end my suspicions and boost my pride in playing the piece. I wasn't gonna be fooled.

I stared at him dubiously.

"I thought you'd assign some baroque or classical stuff. My junior high teacher once mentioned 'The Dead March from Saul, Samson and Israel in Egypt.' He said that was about the best piece ever composed for trombone. I thought I'd be playing stuff like that for you."

Gluey paused for a moment to think about the Dead March. "I've played it, of course." Gluey seemed impressed that I knew the name of a famous piece, but I definitely got the impression he did not plan to assign that.

"What about that? The Dead March thing?" I pressed him.

"You don't really want to play that, do you?" He sounded weary.

"Sure, I do," I lied. I was being a snot, frankly.

"I'd like you to play happier things. I prefer music to be jolly."

By that, apparently, he meant screamers, straight out of the old circus line-up. Jeez.

He seemed to think the worst was over, that I had capitulated. "You're going to need double and triple tonguing in these measures. Have you done much tonguing, James?"

"Not really, sir." I felt fed up with him.

Gluey ignored my obvious anger. "The syllables you say is ta and ka and you make it with the tip of the tongue touching the palate just above the top front teeth. I have a very famous book, a used copy, for you to borrow until you get the hang of it, and some practice sheets here for you to try during your practice time. These are free of charge to you."

"Thank you," I said coldly.

"Circus marches, screamers, are faster than a normal military march and usually are played at about 130 to 150 beats per minute. You'll need to play fast on this one."

"I don't know if I can manage that."

"You probably can't now. You'll have to work on it, of course. It's going to take a while to get you up to pace. There's a lot to teach you. Can you play 'The Stars and Stripes Forever?'"

"I have played that, sir. A few times."

"Good. Do you still have the music?"

"Possibly. I'm pretty sure I do."

He wrote that down in a notebook he had. "Excellent. In the next month I'll want you to show me you know it by heart. That's a useful piece of music."

Useful? It might be if you were in a military band, which was very uncool. He didn't explain what possible use I might have for it.

At this point I was wondering whether he thought I was no good as a musician or something. Or maybe he thought I was a kid and would want to play music that sounded like clowns and elephants dancing around. Adults have some really stupid ideas of what teenagers like. Sure, I'd played plenty of Souza in band class, but I hadn't expected something lighthearted and silly like a crappy circus piece, man. It would be fun, but it wasn't what you expect from a guy who went to Juilliard. You have to agree. You don't expect circus crap.

I looked over the piece he had put in front of me. It had measures with a lot of down and up slides, glissandos, which is the way they do it for silly sounds. Bwaa-upppp, you know. I could tell it was crazy music the minute he put it on the music stand in front of me and at the top it had instructions in Italian to play it like a circus. That was another clue.

While I was looking at the notes and trying to make out what he meant by assigning me that piece, I had the strange feeling that Gluey was examining me, especially my head! I glanced out of the corner of my eye at him, but didn't say anything. I don't like confronting people directly about stuff like that, when they're being rude and things. I always figure they will stop soon enough and pretty soon I'm going to know what was bothering them. I know I'm not a great looking person, but I didn't think I was a goddamned freak or anything. Why was he giving me the once over? The creeps was what he was giving me, to tell you the truth, and I was wondering what in the world could be wrong with my head. My hair wasn't dirty or anything. I wasn't a comic book horror. He seemed to want to ask me something, but I waited for him to decide to do it. I didn't look his way. That way he wouldn't know that I had seen him peering at me.

"But... you like your hair long, James?" said Gluey finally, examining my ears. It felt to me as though something awful was crawling out of my head. Like I had head lice or gobs of shiny dark brown earwax oozing out for everyone to gawk at. He seemed genuinely curious to know what I thought.

I felt self-conscious and blushed. "Huh?" was my reply.

Gluey had a crew cut himself, then it dawned on me that he might not like the length of my hair, which is an issue with some older people, of course. Ever since young people have been growing their hair long, after the fashion of the Beatles, comments have been coming at those of us who dig even slightly longish hair, and mine is not that long compared to many. There are even people who will glare at you and call you names in public. Adults who will do that. These crew cut people can get uptight about even a slightly long crew cut.

"You like your hair the way you have it now? Down below your ears?" Gluey continued.

I frowned at him. Before this Gluey hadn't seemed the type to dwell on the personal aspects of a young person's appearances. I was shocked and I wondered what he was getting at. I figured he had a crew cut because he was balding at the temples so severely that he would have looked very strange with longer hair. He'd be something out of Dickens, the very picture of a creepy undertaker.

"I have to tell you, James, almost all the men in the Shriner bands are very conservative and they don't like any long-haired hippie boys."

"But sir!" I gasped in horror, "I'm not going to be playing in the Shriner band! Did you think I wanted to be in the Shriner band? There must be a mistake or something. Maybe there's been a misunderstanding. I...I don't know what my mother told you, but um, I'm just taking lessons from you so I can be in the high school band, sir. At my high school! My new director wrote us a letter that said we all had to take private lessons from someone this summer if we wanted to be in the band. That's why I'm here. I don't know anything about the Shriner band. I think you have to be an adult to be one of them. They're real old guys." The idea that he thought I was going to be in a Shriner band horrified me. I'd seen Shriners in the parades, driving crazy loud little cars and looking stupid with Dumbo the Elephant hats on their heads. I didn't know much about them, except that they were ancient and incredibly stupid.

Gluey shifted uncomfortably in his chair and didn't look me in the eyes. "Well, James, I happen to play first chair trombone in the Shriner band, and I really enjoy it. The problem I have here is, if you continue taking lessons with me, I might need some more trombones to flesh out the band. I think I might have to call on you to sub in the Shriner band as another lower chair in the trombone section. Only the best kids that I teach get called and I think you might be one of the best ones this year, James. I'll know after you show me your double and triple tonguing work over the next couple of months. And some pedal tones. I won't say you'll make it in the Shriners and I won't say it's absolutely required for you to help me, however if I ask someone they've always cooperated. Always. You're one of the ones right now that I'm teaching who can read music, at least. If I can teach you to double and triple tongue, you'll be useful to me. If we're lacking tubas, I may use you for the deep notes. In the past I have hardly ever had to, but things are different this year and I might. Have to. The Shriners are volunteers and our circuses are for crippled kids, kids with cleft palates and burns, you see? It's sad but we're not getting that many to participate in the band, especially late this spring and next year. I'm anticipating losing a few old time players next year to age and health, too."

Oh, boy, talk about pulling the old sob story. Get out your goddamned handkerchief. Sheesh! Crippled kids are going to miss out. Old guys are dying all over the place. Heck, what had I gotten into? I knew those Shriner guys were really, really old. That would be a goddamned blast playing with a bunch of old farts.

I was in such a panic mentally that I could barely think of a lie to get me out of that crap. Frantically, inside my brain, I was casting around for something that would work. I thought maybe I ought to claim to have some kind of deadly illness that would make it impossible for me to play trombone a lot in a week, but that seemed difficult to prove. I did have a light case of asthma, occasionally. I wondered if I ought to bring that up and exaggerate the diagnosis.

"Sir," I said gravely, "I have asthma attacks. I had to go to the Asthma Clinic and wrap my chest with thick rubber and tickle myself with a brush on a motorized cocktail mixer and go to these lessons with other kids where we run across the room..." I realized this true story about the various treatments I had undergone for asthma was pretty ridiculous, not to mention poorly explained, but I was really feeling hysterical at that point.

"Oh, I've heard you playing James, and even with asthma you can blow fine. You've got plenty of breath," said Gluey, shooting this down quickly.

This Shriner thing was coming at me out of left field. I didn't know what to say next. I've never been much good at coming up with a series of good lies on the spur of the moment.

"I think my mother and my father better hear this. I don't think they're gonna like it." I was buying time until I could think of a reason why my mother wasn't gonna like it. Several possibilities occurred to me.

Gluey shrugged. "Okay, James, I think that would be a

very good idea. Tell your mother what I said," replied Gluey, as though it wasn't going to make a bit of difference and he knew it. I wondered if he'd already told her about this Shriner requirement. I had a sneaking suspicion about that.

I suddenly had what I thought was an inspired bolt of brilliance. My mother had been complaining that my grades were slipping and I never did any yard work at home. She wanted me to rake the gravel in the front yard. I would use that as an excuse to get me out of the Shriners.

"Mom'll have to agree to me going anywhere on Saturdays. She's real picky about me doing anything outside school, because of chores and homework and stuff. Algebra is going awful terrible for me right now and I can't graph a thing right so far, because I have a real dork as a teacher and all he does is draw pests from his State pest test. And also, I don't think she'll agree to let me go anywhere that's too far, because she worries something awful if I even spend the night at a friend's house, or, maybe she won't let me go anywhere at all. Come to think of it, she wants me to do lots of chores around the house this year, too. She says I'm about her laziest child and I have to change before she sends me out in the world." I knew as I said all this that I was sounding more and more like a ridiculous kid, but I didn't care. The thought of playing in the Shriners band was the pits. I couldn't even stand thinking about it for a second. I was praying Mom wouldn't want me to go anywhere. I was praying for lots of chores to come my way and for mother to remember how worried she said she was about my grades.

"Well, I'm sorry to hear that," said Gluey calmly, "but if you take lessons with me that'll be the understanding. I use the boys who study with me as subs in the Shriner band, so I guess I'll explain that to her, and I think she'll agree."

Of course, when Mom came for me that day I didn't mention anything that Gluey said about the Shriner band, and how he wanted to recruit me. I've always believed that it's better to let sleeping dogs snooze, as they say. If worse came to worse, I could pretend to be really bad at double and triple tonguing, though

I knew in my heart that I wasn't the type of person who could pretend to be a boob.

CHAPTER FOUR

I suppose some of you wise ass-listeners are giggling to yourselves and can probably just about guess what happened to me next. Yeah, yeah, it's obvious you'll say, seeing into the Forces That Be in your infinite wisdom. Ho, ho, damn you. In the next episode of the Great Adult Conspiracy against James, Gluey actually called my mother a few weeks later, my freshman year in high school. It had been a couple of weeks and I foolishly thought that Gluey was not going to call for me or I'd told him enough ridiculous excuses why I couldn't volunteer that he'd been discouraged about my willingness. Nothing could have been further from the truth. He'd only been biding his time before striking.

"Oh, hello," said Mother with surprise as she picked up the telephone receiver one evening.

I was suspicious about her surprise and I immediately got up from my desk and tiptoed out to the hall so I could eavesdrop on her end of the conversation. Our phone sat on top of the upright piano in one corner of that '60s living room I told you about, and you could stand in the hall without anyone seeing you and hear everything that was said on our end of the phone.

"Uh huh," said Mother, "I think that is a wonderful opportunity for our Jimmie."

Oh my god, I thought. Gluey had done it. He'd asked if I could play with the Shriner band and Mom was agreeing!

"We don't object. Jimmie needs something to do on his weekends."

Oh great, she wasn't even asking me if I wanted to!

Gluey made his request of me to be allowed to substitute in the Shriner band from time to time, as he put it, for circuses and parades, riding on the Shriner bus to remote towns, and my mother explained that her rules about chores and doing things out of school, strangely enough, did not apply to torturous stuff like playing for the Shriner band on the weekend. Yeah, you guessed it. Oh no, according to my mother playing for the Shriner band was perfectly okeydokey with her, in fact, the more playing time with the Shriners the better, she thought. My old man, it turned out, had been in DeMolay, and knew all about black balling people, and the Ancient Arabic Order of the Nobles of the Mystic Shrine, or A.A.O.N.M.S., also known as the goddamned Shriners, and junk like that, and he thought my helping the Shriners was boss and a cool thing for me to be doing in my spare time. Crippled children, tears, wonderful, of course, our son will be playing in the band to help!

Notice, my parents weren't helping any crippled children themselves. No way, Jose. Mom even called Gluey back after talking with my father and assured Gluey that he shouldn't hesitate to call on me for anything at all. I was hearing her end of this whole conversation between them and moaning in quiet agony. As far as I was concerned, I was doomed. She said I was taking lessons from him, therefore I was going to have to replace trombones in the Shriner band as soon as he thought I was good enough.

And I had to keep my hair no longer than the bottom of my ear lobe. Because my hair was completely straight, it was easy for them to see how long it really was. I wanted to grow it to my shoulders, but now that had gone out the window. I was my parents' robot, without a will of my own, it seemed.

On the first day of school when I was in my new band class, I stood in line to give my instructor the receipts from my lessons with Gluey. "I've got a whole stack," I said to the guy in front of me, showing him my pile. He had stooped shoulders and a huge wad of small papers pinched in his hand. Receipts, similar to mine.

"Me too," he responded.

"Hey, do we have to keep going to lessons?" I asked, fishing for more information without asking my band director who I knew would say I ought to continue with lessons simply for the love of music.

"I'm not," said the boy. "I think you only have to give these in once, before your freshman year."

By then I had reached the front of the line. The band director took the pile of receipts, wrapping a rubber band around them, without even glancing at the dates or anything. He put a check beside my name in his grade book! I sensed that this was all my teacher required and perhaps after I was in the band I didn't have to continue taking lessons. I asked around some more to see if other people besides the boy in line had the same idea. They agreed that this band instructor only required the lessons before the first year, after that you didn't have to keep providing receipts. Nothing required me to go on for the entire school year!

I went home that day and I tried subtlety to explain the facts to Mom, but she said she thought I ought to go on with lessons. Gluey believed I had real talent. Talent! Goddammit! Talent to play for a bunch of clowns! I knew he only wanted me for the Shriner band. I was being used as a fill-in for a band because they couldn't get anyone else to do it and my parents were perfectly copasetic with that!

As soon as I got this response from Mom I decided something would have to be done, and done quickly. I had a feeling that these private lessons would lead to a lot of Saturdays and Sundays spent volunteering for the Shriners, something that I didn't want. I had to get out of those private lessons before a date when he asked me to play for the Shriner band. I didn't want to be hanging out with a lot of conservative old coots in my spare time. They were probably hawks who loved Nixon or something! I didn't know exactly what their main mission or idea was, but I was working on being cooler and I figured this Shriner stuff was not going to help. That was when I cooked up the idea of claiming that there was something mysterious about Gluey. Damn, the truth was I was trying anything to get my mom to think trombone lessons were a bad idea.

I recalled my initial reaction to the size of the house and the fact that he had me pay in cash. I'm embarrassed to admit it, but I decided to use those to cook up some kind of doubts about Gluey. I can see now that it was sorta a dumb-ass thing to do.

"Mom, the way Mr. McGluen hides his family is really weird," I said as casually as I could a little while after I had arrived home from the next lesson.

"What do you mean?" asked Mom. "Everyone who gives private lessons in their home keeps their family out of the way. It wouldn't be professional to let their family stroll in and out during lessons."

"But I didn't even hear them once."

"There wasn't a car in the garage," mother pointed out quickly. "His wife and child must have gone out before we came for your lesson. There's nothing weird about that. Most music teachers do that."

I gulped and tried again. "But he's pretending he doesn't have a wife and a kid, you see. He never mentioned them to me. And there's no name on his mailbox. Do you think he could be wanted? Maybe in Mexico or something?"

"Are you crazy?"

"What about the mailbox?" I asked.

"He probably didn't get around to painting his name on it. Not everybody has their name on their mailbox. In fact, a lot of people don't."

I realized I was going to have to think fast to outsmart my mother, who was not falling for my bullshit. "But you have to pay him in cash," I pointed out. I was trying to make my mother think that paying in cash had strange vibes.

"Oh, that's nothing. You're being ridiculous," Mother scoffed.

I struck back quickly: "Why are you sending me to a man who only accepts cash, mom? The girls got to go to piano lessons and Miss Rich's tap dance lessons and you paid with a check."

(That reminds me of the fact that she had actually tried to have me take tap dancing lessons, too, years earlier, but I had thrown a major fit about it. "Boys do not take tap dance lessons!" I had yelled. At least my old man had backed me up on the truth of that.)

"Some people like cash," Mom claimed.

"Maybe he can't get a bank account, Mom. Maybe there's something really, really wrong! He went to Juilliard and so why is he living in that dinky little house? I thought that was suspicious, right from the start. Why is he so cheap for lessons? That just doesn't make sense. That's what I wonder..." It was true that Gluey didn't charge as much as he could have for lessons. Three dollars was cheap. Being a graduate of Juilliard and playing for some of the best swing bands in the west should have made him a super expensive trombone teacher. That would be why my parents picked him. The thing about his lessons was he had that sneaky, ulterior motive. The damn Shriner band!

"James, you're going to continue in lessons," Mom said coolly.

She was getting fed-up. My ridiculous arguments had irritated her and she wasn't listening anymore. I decided in desperation to try a bit of reverse psychology on her. "Oh, gosh, I'm not saying I want to drop lessons with him, Mom. If I had to drop trombone lessons it would be awful, just terrible! I don't know what I'd do with my spare time! Please Mom, don't make me stop lessons. I don't think he's really dangerous or anything. I just don't know if it's safe," I said.

"Listen carefully, James Eldritch Sauerbaugh. You are going to continue trombone lessons. Mr. McGluen says you're talented." Use of my full name meant I was entering dangerous territory.

Since reverse psychology hadn't worked, I returned to my original argument. "Okay, okay, but the whole thing screams wanted fugitive if you ask me and if you have half the woman's intuition you claim you'll—"

"James, you'll continue lessons." She was getting rather brutal at that point; I knew it was time to quit.

◆ ◆ ◆

So getting out of lessons was impossible. I was doomed to continue and face the possibility of being recruited for the Shriner Band. Unless I never learned double or triple tonguing. The trouble was I actually liked learning those techniques.

Starting that November, Gluey had me listen to some of his music. You guessed it—all of what he played for me was circus music. We heard an LP with "The Circus Bee" and another one which had "Rolling Thunder." Gluey gave me pointers on what to listen for during the music, which were the trombone parts, fast, slow or deep. And over the course of the winter months, Gluey assigned me a lot of trombone duets. Sometimes he would take the fast part and I would take a slow, low melodic part. The next time he would switch and have me try the fast tempo. I was rather bad at it, and not even deliberately, either.

"Do you know your double and triple tonguing? We'll need that for this piece," he would warn.

Practice work for double and triple tonguing would be saying my little syllable sounds, ta and ka, sort of in a mumbo-jumbo chant like a zombie in a comic book coming to get you. I said these chants out loud to him. Ta-ta-ka, ta-ta-ka, ta-ka, ta-ka, ta-ka. Like that. And ta-ka, ta-ka, ta-ka, ta-ta-ka, ta-ta-ka.

Then another thing he did was he showed me some alternate positions with the slide that I might use to play a few of the fastest screamers. I was lousy at those. He worked me on pedal tones for a few weeks, extra low and obnoxious, because they might not have enough tubas. I understood the tuba guys were too old and couldn't blow hard without keeling over. I liked pedal tones a lot.

His favorite thing to drill into me over and over was that "the music demanded light tongue, driven by air."

In the early spring I played tons of music alone, not in duets. He assigned "Entrance of the Gladiator" by Julius Fucik, which is also known as "Thunder and Blazes." That pieces just booms away; it's really boss. Of course we worked on "Barnum and Bailey's Favorite," by Karl King. That guy wrote hundreds of goddamned screamers. Gluey laid on a lot of Jewell and Fillmore, of course, because they're sort of mandatory in circus land. I had to practice playing everything forte, because for circuses you had to play damn loud to be heard over the chugging motorcycles and trumpeting elephants and the screaming kids. I was blasting Gluey's little living room. I'm surprised the paint-by-number clown paintings didn't fall off his damn moss green walls. At home when I practiced, Ginny complained about the noise, but my parents defended anything I did for Mr. McGluen.

"Your muscle memory for triple tonguing will come with a slower tempo," Gluey explained. So we played some slower things.

The next week he assigned *"Sobre las Olas,"* that's "Over the Waves" for those of you who don't know Spanish, if you haven't been in Sr. O'Shaunnessey's class, and that's the song that they use for the trapeze acts. Come to think of it, I probably listened to it on an LP first in Gluey's living room. It's an old thing that they always play for circuses and everybody knows that old swaying thing.

"Everyone assumes it was written by Strauss," Gluey said, "but I'm pretty proud to tell you that it was written by a Mexican. A great composer named Juventinos Rosas. He was a natural composer, a street musician who wrote many dances, polkas, schottisches, and this famous circus piece. It was available on a Wurlitzer so it became popular. He was a very talented man but he died at age 26 on tour in Cuba." Gluey was a big booster for Mexican people and junk. I never really figured out why, but maybe his wife was from there.

Next, Gluey taught me the B-flat chord as a stinger, he called it.

"Ta-daa, onomatopoetically in English, is what you need to play when someone or an animal finishes a big trick successfully. It's the flourish. The conductor signals it this way." Gluey illustrated different signs of what the conductor might do to call for a stinger.

So I got more parade and circus music. More than I can tell you. Yeah, heck, I knew for sure then that he was trying to train me to play for the goddamned Shriner's circus and parade band and nothing else. There was no classical music at all. He was charging my mother fees to train me to play in the circuses. Juilliard be damned. It didn't feel right. I was being set up to perform for the clowns.

I was angry. I knew he meant well; Shriners was a charity. But somehow it didn't seem fair when he knew, or could have guessed from the way I acted, that I hated the idea of playing for circuses.

My Algebra teacher my freshman year—the goofy man who went along with my textbook—was an extremely irresponsible person by the name of Lincoln Faber and he was a crack-up as a teacher, let me tell you. Totally goofy. Hell, every day in his class was funny.

He was the tannest man you've ever seen. And he had this enormous tan forehead. One of the kids in class said you could write the entire lyrics of everything Jim Morrison sang in "Light My Fire" on Lincoln Faber's forehead, but he was so tan you wouldn't be able to read it. "Light My Fire" is about a half an hour long or something. Sheesh. Mr. Faber had lost half his hair and the other half was a shimmery silver and blonde color. In the summer he wore brown pants. His shirts were plaids, like graph paper. In the winter he always wore a tight navy blue or green V-neck pullover over those shirts.

Leaning like a lazy son-of-a-bitch against the chalk board, Mr. Faber seemed every day to be about to begin to lecture us on the subject he was supposed to teach, Algebra, but that never happened. He always stopped, held the chalk, looked like a damn wizard and then began drawing something slowly on the board, taking a great deal of care.

"What would you say this fellow was, huh?" he challenged the class after he finished the drawing.

We'd all seen this before. He would have carefully drawn this shape, but it wasn't a parabola or some interesting mathematical function. Hell no, it was always an indistinguishable insect. Antennae, six legs, three body parts. A dang bug.

Every day he spent about half of our hour in class showing us the outline of various bugs, pests, which he had to be able to identify for his pest test. He had started a business painting lawns green, but that was failing, so he wanted to change and use similar spraying equipment to spread pesticides. This side business he planned for the weekends and summers and in order to spray pesticides he needed a state certificate. Teaching being such a well-paying profession, he had to have this stupid second job. Over and over he registered for the state test to spray pesticides and over and over he failed it because he couldn't recognize the various bugs. He claimed the reason he kept failing this test was that the mimeograph that went with the test was too watery and pale. He was trying to show us on the chalkboard how watery and pale the mimeo had been. That's the kind of nut this guy was.

Everyone who was awake in third period Algebra would be staring at the crazy drawing of a bug on the chalkboard. In the meantime Faber would be messing around with one of the bug's legs, trying to make it look even more absurd and less bug-like. We'd all roll our eyes at each other behind his back, Faber was doing it again, showing us bug drawings. Where was the

Algebra, the equations, the Cartesian coordinates?

Maybe, we thought, we ought to protest this by not saying anything in response to his question.

"I was like you. No way to tell, right? It isn't clear, is it?" Mr. Faber claimed happily.

We would then be forced to agree that his pest test had been unfair. Yes, we nodded, what he'd drawn on the board didn't look like any particular insect. That was all he wanted to hear.

At that point, he would sometimes go on to teach us some Algebra, in his own special crappy way, sorta as an afterthought like, okay, here's what they pay me to do, take it or leave it and I'm not putting any of my effort into it.

But I liked that class because some of my classmates were strange, too. There was this girl who sat beside me. She was very pretty, long glossy brown hair, cute legs. Always wearing short skirts and tight sweaters, but she never talked to me.

One day that changed. She turned to me and suddenly said, "I'm really afraid about being kidnapped this weekend."

I had no goddamned idea what she was talking about! It was bitchin' that she'd spoken to me, so I just gazed at her sorta cool and boss. Or I tried to do that. My goddamned lips were kinda trembling. I didn't feel brave with my lips doing that, however she musta thought I was brave since she was telling me about her troubles. Was someone threatening her? It sounded weird and wonderful. I was really embarrassed that she was talking to me, especially because that day I had a string of zits across my forehead like a dotted line to show where you needed to open my head for repairs or something and I didn't want her looking too closely at me. (She did have some zits herself, but much smaller ones near her nose, which was as oily as a homemade taco. My eyesight is bad, but I could see the shine

"We have to leave the front door unlocked next Friday night and they're coming to get me at about 4 am. Isn't that awful early?"

"Huh?" I said. It seemed peculiar to complain about the hour of your kidnapping. I was beginning to think she was what my

Grandma Sauerbaugh would have called "ex-ta persnickety."

"I got into cheerleaders," she added by way of explanation.

"What the hell do you mean?" I asked politely.

"I'm going to get kidnapped. For a kidnap breakfast? You know?"

"Oh." I suddenly realized what she'd been talking about. I'd heard of those strange rituals where some of the members of the club you joined drove to your house in the middle of the night and came in your unlocked door to your bedroom and woke you up and took you to a pancake restaurant for breakfast. A bunch of new kids would have this happen to them every spring. I thought the whole thing was great for dip-shits.

"I'm going to find out where they're taking me."

"Okay," I played along with her.

"It's going to be so exciting!"

The bell rang and I left the conversation at that.

The next day she started in on the same dumb topic again. I was a little excited that she was talking to me once more, but the kidnap breakfast bored me.

"Do you want to know where they're taking me for the kidnap breakfast?" she asked.

"Not really," I said in all honesty.

"I'm not supposed to know," she said in a dumb-o whisper, "but it's gonna be Bob's Big Boy."

"Oh yeah. Pancakes and crap."

She looked a little shocked by the curse word. "I guess. I don't like going places in my pajamas," she added.

"Sheesh, that's uncool being in pajamas. Sleep in your clothes."

"Yeah, I want to, but my mom won't let me and I hate it. I'm wearing shoes, no slippers, no way. I'm going to hide my slippers so I can't possibly wear them."

"Yeah, do that." I was getting a little tired of this kidnap breakfast topic. I'd never been disappointed by talking with a girl before, except Ginny. It was a new experience and kinda educational. I'd always thought pretty girls would be fascinating, but this one was so damned boring. I'd never talked to anyone as boring as her in my entire life. It was worse than that, really. Talking to her was like opening a hideous trunk—like Pandora's Box. For two days she had chatted to me about kidnapping and there seemed to be no end of her yakking on the subject.

The next day, a third day in a row, she started in for another go on that same dumb topic. "I'm pretty sure my mom is going to suggest I wear my slippers when I'm kidnapped," she bitched.

"Okay," I said sullenly. I got the definite feeling she was talking really loud so other people could hear that she was in cheerleaders. This day I noticed she was sorta casting her eyes around in the direction of the in crowd to see if her amusing words were having much of an effect on them.

"She's probably going to tell me to put my hair in pigtails or something cute when I'm going to bed before I'm kidnapped. I don't want to look like a kid with all the cheerleaders!" I caught her sneaking a glance at an in crowd guy nearby. She was talking loud enough for him to hear.

"Ah huh," I said kinda slow and disgusted-like at her.

She was picking up my angry vibes. "I think them coming into my house is kinda creepy. What do you think?" She tried to act truly fascinated by my opinion.

"Yeah. I can dig it. Oh, by the way, are you experienced?" That was a thing you asked girls to embarrass them, but you were talking about Jimi Hendrix's album.

"Huh?" She looked shocked. The in crowd guy snorted loudly.

"Have you heard *The Jimi Hendrix Experience*?" I asked, trying suavely to get off the pancake breakfast topic.

"No, but my sister has it. But have you ever been kidnapped?"

There was that damned pancake breakfast kidnapping again! I'd had it with kidnapping. "No, I haven't, but they're pretty much for shit heads. Maybe we should listen to Faber." The in crowd guy cracked up again when I said kidnap breakfasts were for shit heads.

I really didn't need Faber to teach me though, I read my school books carefully. I did that a lot before the circuses and the parades. But I'm getting ahead of myself.

CHAPTER FIVE

During the months following my first lesson with Gluey, my little sister Ginny loved to tease me about the trombone. She probably was mad about the spit valve torture I gave her, and she knew that I didn't want to go to lessons or be in high school band. However the teasing increased when the month of February, my freshman year, rolled around. You see February meant the annual rodeo parade, *La Fiesta De Los Vaqueros*. As you may recall, it was my wondrous future appearance on TV during that rodeo parade that had caused my damned mother to make me stay in high school band after all. The big parade day arrived, and I was marching, just like every other high school bandsman in town.

About six-thirty in the goddamned a.m.—and it is very dark at that hour even in Arizona—Mom and Ginny drove me to the park where the parade staging grounds were located. After carefully criticizing my appearance (she commented with real disappointment on the breakouts on my forehead and chin and volunteered to let me use her powder in her compact to cover the zits!) Mom pulled the Plymouth up to a curb across from the park and under a street light. My trombone and I split. I left the case in the backseat of the car. As my mom prepared to pull away, Ginny screamed through the closed window, "We'll be watching the whole parade!" Her face, thrust against the glass, gave me a goofy thumbs-up with her eyes crossed and her mouth slack like a goon.

I was about to yell something really sarcastic to Ginny, but from one glance at Mom's face I could tell she was so happy to think she was going to actually see her son appearing on the fabulous boob tube. I felt sorry for her and knew I shouldn't use the occasion to get nasty. It was better to see a live person than to see them on a television set, and she had some nutty notions, but I decided to be nice and humor her.

"Okay, okay!" I called back. "You guys keep a look out for me."

"Be sure and smile!" Mom shouted. "We'll all be watching!"

At home Mom had laid out this big section of the newspaper which listed the order of parade goons and she had clearly marked my number so that she would know when to watch for me. Every group in the parade had an assigned number and the announcers would say the number and the viewer could keep up with what was coming next. Everybody who watched the parade had one of those parade lists handy so they knew when their friends or family members would appear on screen. It was a long list of ding-a-lings like prancing ponies and ladies in horse drill teams or members of a prominent family of morons riding in a rotten old stagecoach. Go West, young moron.

Holy moly, where Mom had dropped me off, near the staging point at a park near downtown, I discovered thousands of these parade ding-a-lings milling around in funny western costumes. Boy, that big blob of the rodeo parade nuts and crackpots was hilarious. I never saw so many mules, creepy cowboys, arthritic imitation sheriffs, horses, oxen, broken-down carriages, dirty donkeys, and precision drill teams. Though I didn't want to be in the band, I have to admit that parade made the whole thing worthwhile. It was like being part of a giant insane snake or something.

Everything corny and stupid showed up for this parade, proving the Wild West to be an amazing collection of crap. A lot of people dressed up as typical Wild West characters with parasols and gun belts. The parade also displayed the Indian tribes of Arizona, though I didn't really care much about them to be honest. Even real Sonoran cowboys were strutting around. Oh boy, they were about as stupid as American cowboys. Maybe stupider! They certainly preferred higher heels!

There were masses of high school bands and baton twirlers throwing their batons into the cold, bare branches of the park trees. This park was a goddamned orgy of golden and silver spangles and stinky leather. What I was wearing wasn't much better. Being in the rodeo parade meant I had to dress like some kind of idiot cowboy in the whole regalia of western crassness and dumbness. My costume screamed "I am a stupid kid pretending to be a damn cowboy!" My band director had decided that year that we had to wear his idea of the traditional school rodeo parade uniform, which consisted of this dorky white shirt, any cowboy hat we had at home (and most of us had one of those) and a red kerchief knotted at our necks. (That kerchief was so you had an uncomfortable neck and a big triangle of funny looking fabric hanging off the front of you as though you were wearing a bib.) Of course, we had to wear jeans and for shoes, tennis shoes or cowboy boots, if we had them. That was a bad looking costume, lemme tell you. In it, I looked to be the biggest jerk, an all-around idiot goat-roper of semi-normal intelligence. I'll say the one nice thing about our cowboy costume was that we didn't have to wear white gloves, the bands in traditional uniforms had on those prissy things.

Big old mansions of the rich railroad men surrounded that park. Someone painted them bright colors like yellow and turquoise and the same jerks had probably transplanted saguaro cactuses in the dirt yards. Near one of those old homes, guys with headbands were sitting on a volcanic stone wall laughing at us, laughing at the whole parade. I'm pretty sure those guys were stoned. I can still see their dilated pupils looking over at us and joking back and forth. It was so embarrassing to be part of that parade when I saw those guys.

By this time the mountains were going purplish to the north and the sun was burning its way over the eastern mountains. A light breeze shuffled a paper toward me. I was feeling sad about how dumb I looked when I noticed some guys who wanted to march in the parade in protest of the war and they were arguing with the parade marshals at a table in a corner of the park. One of them had on army fatigues. They all had headbands, woven ones from Mexico, beards, long hair, mustaches or goatees, and dark glasses. A couple of them wore cool olive drab jackets and kerchiefs on their heads, which was cooler than wearing them at your neck. Of course they all wore bellbottoms and boots and even leather sandals, though the morning was pretty cold and windy. There was a girl with them in striped pants that were tucked into her boots. She was so sexy looking.

I tried to listen in to see if they were going to be allowed in the parade. I guess they didn't get a permit and the marshal wasn't going to give them one, because they had to be in western dress. They decided to walk at the very back of the parade and there wasn't much the authorities could do about that. Apparently it was still a free country. Who'da thunk?

Within minutes a couple of cowboy jerks began yelling curses at the protesters and they had to move away. Of course these cowboys had never been anywhere near a war. I'm sure they were in the National Guard or something, but from the look of them, not college deferred. There is no way they would go to college unless it was to major in Ag. They were both probably former members of the Future Farmers of America, an organization of goons who like to grow goats.

Cowboy-type people mostly support the war in Vietnam, which is a really uncool thing about them that people don't know, except those of us who actually know them. They are really gung-ho about killing people. They like beating up hippie kids almost as much as they like beating up blacks and Mexicans and Papago Indians who they happen to find wandering around in the wrong place. If they found a long-haired type, they would stomp him and cut his hair off and scream stuff at him like "fairy!" or "dirty Indian." The hippies living out in the middle of nowhere in Arizona have to be really carefully of cowboys, young or old—they're nothing but trouble. They are considered the goons of the west by the rest of us, just a roving band of dangerous dickheads waiting to make life difficult for other people. They like their hair in crew cuts and they want everybody to conform. That's it really, they are goddamned conformists, which is strange given the fact that the original cowboys weren't that at all, or maybe, come to think of it, they were. I guess it's fake that the original cowboy was all for freedom. He might have been for his own freedom, however I'll bet he wanted to herd the rest of us around. Get it, herd us? The modern ones sure don't want any hippie stuff. What they love is Richard Nixon and the flag. All this stuff about cowboys being so great is a bunch of hooey and crap. A parade to honor them? Ho, ho, ho.

◆ ◆ ◆

Those of us lucky enough to be in the trombones were at the front of my school band, of course, leading the band, as in the popular musical with 76 trombones and all that garbage. That being the case the camera would catch sight of us first after the drum majors. I didn't like any of our drum majors. Talk about bossy people! They ordered everyone around and showed off non-stop. That morning before the rodeo parade began, one of them was jumping off a volcanic stone wall over and over and screaming "Can you dig it?" The band director wisely was threatening him with various punishments, to no damn effect.

Eventually, the goddamned show organized itself and we took off into the brisk cold sunshine, marching in the rotting streets of downtown, by the Old Pueblo's bars, courthouses, sad department stores, and failing shoe stores. I remember some clerks standing under the striped awnings, waving and smiling in the morning sun. Outside a bunch of hotels, well-dressed tourists acted serious. I remember a few large women in fur, and their balding husbands in suits and Homburgs with bola ties at their necks. Old ladies in squaw dresses and suede jackets applauded us with their big penny purses from Mexico flapping around. Straw cowboy hats on old men and little babies. Tilting in every damn direction. You could see big old lumps of turquoise belt buckles on fat men in saddle pants, and fake mustaches on young men in serapes and sombreros. Laughing policemen held back boys who pointed silver revolvers at us. Far away, blue and purple mountains sat sorta quiet watching us pass the Indian shops and pawnshops full of Hopi jewelry and Navajo rugs.

All around me in the parade itself, donkeys brayed, mules snorted. Old wagons were creaking and swaying ahead of us in a long line. The strange sickly sweet smell of cotton candy drifted in the breeze. The conquistadores, cowboys and crappy clowns smiled and waved. Horse drill teams pranced behind a shiny black Mariah, an undertaker's wagon. Empress Charlotte's coach had Mexican bank clerks lolling out the windows.

Eventually our turn came to be in the TV camera. That was when I got screwed. It just so happened that there was a wagon in front of me drawn by a team of giant bored oxen and one of those big bored oxen had relieved itself—and I do mean relieved itself—in the most massive pile of relieving you can imagine and that pile was right, I mean absolutely directly as possible, in line with me. Of course, the trombones led the band and we are supposed to really make things look sharp and not step the least bit out of line, no matter what. We're trained to walk straight through the manure piles, but if I'd noticed this particular massive dropping I probably wouldn't have stepped directly in it. I'm kinda blindish, you'll recall. So you can imagine this big steaming ox dropping in front of me and imagine me stepping the only place there was to go. In the middle of the biggest pile of ox poop imaginable.

And that was what my whole family saw on television. That was the big family glory that my mother had been waiting for so eagerly. You'll recall the whole reason I was taking trombone in high school was so that I could appear on the TV and my big TV debut had come and gone and it involved ox poop and me stepping into it.

Ginny was especially impressed by my colossal failure and has not since let me forget the look on my face when I stepped right into it. Yeah, and after I stepped I saw the camera and pretty much knew that I had been filmed stepping into it.

"You were out of sight!" said Ginny when she saw me.

Mother was solemn, stiff and sniffy with me when I got into the car and rode home that rodeo noon. I couldn't look her in the eye, though I knew it wasn't my fault. I got busy in the back seat taking my trombone apart and oiling it carefully.

"What's that stinky smell?" asked Ginny a few minutes after I had entered the car.

"Slide oil," I said.

"No, I mean the other smell."

"Flake off," I said evilly.

I know Mom must have seen me on TV, and I also knew she probably could smell my shoes, even though I had tried to wipe them in the grass in the park when we stopped at the end of the parade. She didn't say anything about the glory of my being on television after that. That was a lost topic. She seemed miffed at me though, as though I'd done it on purpose. I didn't put that pile of dung in front of me, and I had nothing to do with where the camera was and the fact that I'd ended up in a close-up shot. It was the great Forces That Be again conspiring against James Sauerbaugh.

I put my tennis shoes outside the door and cleaned them the next day. Ah well, at least I was able to say I'd appeared once on TV. Oh, and Mom was right; I'm real perky as a result.

CHAPTER SIX

Finally it happened. I dreaded it, but I knew it was gonna hafta happen. The phone rang a couple of weeks after *La Fiesta De Los Vaqueros* and Mom answered it. It was Gluey calling to say that one of his trombonists had left town in an emergency to nurse an ailing brother in New Mexico, and Gluey asked me to substitute in the trombone section of the Shriner band that very weekend.

Lucky me, it turned out that my first concert with the Shriners was at their big annual circus performances which they were putting on for crippled and underprivileged kids in town. It was a yearly springtime thing in most of the towns in Southern Arizona to have a Shriner circus. They always had performances for the underprivileged children on Saturdays early. The evening show was for profit, and they used the proceeds from that for their charities, mostly surgeries for kids with cleft palates and cleft lips and problems walking. My mom left me off at the community center early on the Saturday morning and I was supposed to warm up to play three circuses that day.

Following Gluey's instructions on the phone, I was wearing a disgusting pair of dress slacks and goofy dress loafers, a jerky white button down collared shirt with a conservative tie like I wore at church, but I never went there anymore after confirmation. Not a wide tie, which was popular, but a narrow tie of conservative colors. I looked like a real A-number-one dork extraordinaire. And I had my Algebra book with me. I got to read a lot of it in the hours between the three circuses.

When I got there, the desert sun was up, but it was March

and I felt how cool it was in the shade of the big community center. I hadn't wanted to play for a circus, but now that I was doomed, I was sorta excited about being part of a show until ten at night and my heart was really thumping as I found my way to the entrance for the band performers and circus people. It was kinda exciting being part of the circus instead of being a dumb kid in the audience gaping at elephants and straining to see the dorky man on the trapeze. Elephants and James were in the circus together now. I was part of the circus scene. Can you dig it? I guess every kid wants to run away with the circus, and here I was being a part of it, if only a Shriner circus and if only in the dumb band. I was really feeling kinda cool about being a circus backstager, and a little scared about my musical abilities. I'm kinda into honesty at the moment.

The people who were around seemed sorta tough and blasé. I guess these performers were failures in regular big circuses and had to be in the Shriner's crappy circus for a lot lower pay. Their costumes were a little sad, faded and less than perfect. One of the jerky trapeze guys looked like something out of the twenties. A whole lot of their glitter was gone from their suits, and their makeup was badly applied. The minute they were out of the ring they dropped their performer's persona and got snappy and bored. Some of the trapeze flyers bit their nails and gossiped. Those were not very sexy looking ladies, up close, either. They could have been cleaning ladies in a goddamned motel or lunch ladies. The animal trainers chewed gum. There was crappy paint on props and a worn look to this circus, but I was a performer and that made it special. Though they were a sad bunch, they were circus people anyway. I tried to look blasé, too, to fit in with the tough, workman-like crowd.

I passed a guy with yappy little dogs and crabby llamas. Some more trapeze flyers in goofy slippers walked by, waddling a little, and I could hear the elephants trumpeting. The arena was laid out in three ring, of course. Motorcycles chugged by with dogs stacked on the back and everywhere there was a lounging, evil-smelling crew moving dirty wooden boxes for the elephant to do tricks on.

Then I had to stroll by the Shriner clowns. They had these loud clown cars, with lawn mower engines smoking and belching blue fumes. Blech! One of them had a gigantic wind-up key in the side, of course. That was the one the clowns were gonna crowd into, natch. They were hanging around waiting to hop into their goofy cars. Fake Ferraris and Corvette Stingrays. These clowns specialized in looking horribly creepy. A wrinkly old clown is something you don't want to get up close to, no matter how much makeup is on their face and these clowns were very old and stiff. They were grouchy and sour and rather nasty. And they all smoked cigarettes and stared at me as though they had some kind of disturbing knowledge they wanted to give me. I've never liked clowns and this close-up encounter increased my hatred of them. They were just creepy. I don't even think they liked young people much, given the way they glared at me.

The Shriner band though, when I saw them—shoot, I can't even describe my shock.

The first thing is they were ancient. They were so old that they resembled Biblical characters, the kind that lived beyond the century mark or the two century mark even! Some of these old guys were fat and some were horribly thin. Some were bald or wore crew-cuts like Gluey and a few had weedy, greasy hair flying in the air in all directions. There were red-faced guys and gray-faced guys. As I got closer I could see all of them had veiny hands and hairy ears. A few of the tall Shriners were stooped. Hard of hearing, mostly (I kid you not!), and the conductors had a difficult time getting their attention.

The thing that scared me was how low in energy they seemed. I wondered how they were going to be able to play well, not to mention playing at all or staying awake or alive. I worried frankly whether some of them could even hold up their instruments for the minutes it would take to play a typical screamer. They looked like a sleeping band, a worn-out tangle of wrinkles. It was like an old German story my mom had once read me about the army that this king named Barbarossa led inside the mountain. They were found centuries later all asleep in various poses around a big old tables. Dead to the world with long, long beards, mostly white. Shriner band members, to a tee.

In the midst of this band of ancients, I noticed there were two other teenagers who were about my age, and they were looking about as lost and confused and aggravated as me. One was a percussionist and the other played the trumpet. The Shriner trumpets were made up of two men who were dead ringers for each other with their long, long gray beards. The old guys were putting the mouthpieces into their instruments and it looked like that was going to be too much labor for them. One fellow had his mouth open and was gasping for air like a fish out of water. A few pop-eyed gentlemen, one of them with a coronet, sat carelessly studying the ceiling tiles, smiling benignly, maybe you could say stupidly.

I stood in front of the band for a second until I found the trombone section, and then Gluey. He was the youngest guy there, besides us teenage substitutes. Like all the band, he wore a maroon fez, the fez from the holy city of Fez, Morocco. His had the local chapter of the Shriners written in gold letters. Habbar, it said. His fez had a long black silky tassel which was coming out of the center of the top. Besides the chapter name, the front of the fez had been decorated with a curving scimitar, the sword of war, covered with fake jewels, and dangling below the scimitar and attached to it was something that looked like a Pharaohs head or an Egyptian lady's head and a crescent shape and a star. It was gaudy and ridiculous.

When I'd worked my way over to the trombones through all the old dead guys, Gluey held out a red felt fez, the kind they sold to kids, which was obviously for me to wear. It had a bright yellow tassel on it. I knew I was going to feel silly wearing my kid's version of it with an elephant lifting its leg painted on the front, but I put it on anyway. Well, at least with the fez on I thought I could blend in with the band and if anyone in the audience knew me they wouldn't be able to pick me out.

I put on the kid's fez, and in that moment I felt a little

magical and a little strange. Like I had a secret compartment floating above my head. I know it sounds goofy but I liked the way my bright yellow tassel slipped around at the top; I liked the towering feeling of the felted dome. About the history of the Shriners and what the hat was supposed to mean I plead total dumbness, however.

I was moving my head around with the fez on it when Gluey spoke again.

"This is Moses Grand," he said, introducing me to the other trombone player.

I shook hands with an ancient fellow who stood up shakily.

"Howdy, kid, have a seat beside me," said Moses. "My original last name was Grandikov, but my grandfather made it simple when he came over from Russia to New York. I like it better myself. I'm grand, don't you know!"

I laughed at his joking manner and sat beside him. I put my trombone case in the space between our chairs, but didn't open it just yet. I felt sorta nervous.

Moses Grand was skinnier than imaginable (his trousers were completely loose in the legs and I often wondered if he even had legs—the rippling material made them like the pants of a stilts walker) and he was very shaky in the hand department. And he had one of those long, long white beards, like a thin curtain of combed cotton, except a little yellow in the mustache parts above his mouth. I think the best way to describe him to you is to say that he resembled a very skinny, very shaky Santa Claus, more like the European version they call Father Christmas. His tiny eyes were bluish gray and had a crinkly arc of laugh lines fanning out from the corners. His skin was pink on the cheeks as though he'd been pinched or slapped. He had a very red nose that came to a sharp point.

Watching him in those minutes before we played together for the first time, I remember I didn't see how he could hold his trombone up at all. His slide was sort of easing into notes all of the time, wallowing around the music in a sloshy, blurry fashion. He was searching around like crazy for the music. He kept his lips working constantly and liked to suck on ice. Oh, and he drank like a fish. Alcohol, I mean, not water. That first day he had the smell of liquor on him, and I noticed a rusty tan colored drink stowed under his folding chair. He was reaching down occasionally and applying the drink to his interior. Plenty of lubrication.

Moses was one of the most cheerful members of the band. I'd been afraid the Shriners were going to be hawks about the war or crabby old jerks. This guy seemed completely different than what I had feared. He was a second generation Russian immigrant from New York who had owned a garage in New Haven, Connecticut, but he couldn't take the winters of the East, and he wanted the heat, so:

"I moved out to Arizona in 1952," he explained happily.

"Oh yeah? 1952? I was born a few years later," I said.

"What a coincidence! You could say I was born or reborn then too, by the experience of coming to the Western desert. Who would have thought a Jew would like the desert? Ha! Wonderful cactus. I couldn't believe in saguaros at first. They were like some miracle of God. Very religious things. It was a spiritual experience for me to encounter them for the first time."

"How did you get started doing this?" I asked.

"What? Playing for the Shriners, you mean?"

"Yeah."

"When I was a kid about your age, I played in Yiddish bands. Then I found the Masons and the Shriners. I thought they had a better reason for playing," Moses explained.

"If you pardon me asking, do they let Jewish people in the Masons?" I felt embarrassed to ask that, but I wondered.

"Certainly. That's a common misunderstanding about the Masons and the Shriners. It isn't exclusively Christian. There are many Jewish members."

"I didn't know it."

"A lot of people think that we're excluded, but it's not so."

Moses told me he had three kids, and lots of grandkids. His children stayed on the East Coast for many years, but had eventually followed their Dad to the West and moved to nearby cities in Arizona. With all that family he was a merry man. I was so relieved that I had a cheerful trombonist near me. Not that Gluey was bad or anything, but he wasn't real cheerful, and I came to find out that he was organizing a lot of the Shriner events and didn't have time to visit with me. At least I'd have a nice old man to talk with, if I ended up subbing a lot. Eventually, I liked the looks of most of the other musicians in the band, besides them being old, but Moses was the happiest one by far. They all did seem to be enjoying playing music, though. In a way they all viewed playing for the circus as some of the best moments in their lives. I found this out as I spent more time with them.

After getting my bearings, I laid my case down on its side and snapped open the clasps. I always liked the smell of the interior of my trombone case, the small velvet drawers and the narrow compartments in which you could tuck rags, pencils, and paper. Like the secret cabinets of a weird old scientist. When I first opened my case, I usually stopped to inhale the scent of the warm old blue velvet, and the sweet odor of slide oil, but I didn't that day as I felt nervous. I got busy fitting my instrument together. The more I hurried the worse my nerves got. I was doing everything ham-fisted. A trombone comes in pieces which you have to fit together, two slides, the mouthpiece, and the bell section. Moses was nice and didn't stare at me as I fumbled around and couldn't get any of the slides connected to the bell section correctly. I felt nervous and shaky as though the circus was about to begin and I was in the path of the elephants. This was the biggest crowd I had ever played for and I wasn't sure I was prepared for following the conductor and staying with the music in the dark and the noise. Instead of staring at me, Moses pretended he needed to study the music again. He took a pencil and marked a few passages thoughtfully. I bet he really didn't need to do that at all. He was trying to make me feel more comfortable. With him being busy, he gave me time to settle in to what was going to happen.

Eventually, he turned to me and spoke.

"Are you ready for the circus?" he asked, chuckling, when I had my trombone together. "All set to go and entertain the kids?"

"I hope so," I said. "I guess I know the music we're playing. I practiced the tunes all this week. Maybe I can't play fast enough, and my triple tonguing is a little weak, but I think I know the notes."

"Sure, you know the notes," said Gluey, leaning forward from his chair on the other side of Moses, "I wouldn't have picked you if I thought you'd do poorly. You're going to be fine. Don't worry. Watch the conductor, though." Gluey locked his trombone slide and laid it in his case. He excused himself and went off to talk to a clown about our start time.

"Ever play music for a circus?" asked Moses when Gluey was gone.

"Um, with Gluey only, sir. We played a lot of screamers."

"Well, I want to warn you, James. It's going to get dark and noisy and smelly especially if the elephants fart when they go by. Or the clowns." He said this very seriously, as though he were telling me something completely scientific, like the speed a rocket would take to leave earth's orbit or something he had calculated.

"Okay," I said, dissolving into laughter. "I can dig it, man. Whatever you say."

"Don't laugh. The clown eat a lot of chili dogs. If either the clowns or the elephants fart you won't be thinking it's too funny. Stay away from these clowns. They are the livid plague. And the trapeze artist with teeny slippers is wearing a costume which I swear came from 1884, so don't mess with him. Ever play to such a big crowd before?"

"Never. No." I was still laughing about the clowns and the weird trapeze artist with the old fashioned costume.

"Well, Shriners mostly play to kids at these circuses. We get big, big crowds of screeching kids. And kids can really scream at the circus. We have to play loudly to get the music above the guys selling popcorn in the stands and the shouts of the lion tamers and the non-stop yelling of the crowd, so no delicate puffs coming out of you. Forte, forte, forte. No pianissimo, got it? I'll do my best, but I'm older than sin and most of the toot is out of me."

"Okay."

"If anything goes wrong with the circus, an animal escapes or someone is injured we switch to 'Stars and Stripes Forever', okay? Remember that."

That explained why Gluey had asked me to memorize that piece on the second lesson.

"You're gonna cover for me, okay?" asked Moses.

"Sure." I thought his playing had seemed a little weak.

"We start in about ten minutes," said Gluey, coming back to us from the clown, who seemed to know the start times better than the band.

"Well, keep your eyes on the music and the conductor," Moses continued, "He's pretty good, this guy. This is the sign for a ta-daa," he showed me what Gluey had already shown me, "and you blow the B-flat chord. Watch for Frank on the coronet, he'll play some quick calls between the new melodies." I looked for this Frank guy. Sound asleep. Arms drooping and mouth wide open. He was gonna play some quick calls? Fat chance.

"Music is laid out here for you as I think you've practiced this week. The conductor has final say and will call out numbers if some things change. Hope the lions don't break free and I hope the man on the flying trapeze does not rip that decrepit costume of his."

"That would be scary," I said, laughing hard.

"No kidding!"

"He'll never be able to replace it!" I said.

"One would hope not!" Moses replied and he laughed so hard he had to wipe his eyes.

He reached under his seat and took a big swig of his drink after he had said that. He saw me watching what he was doing.

"Jokey-cola," he said, winking impishly.

"Uh, that's all right," I replied as suavely as I could, "I'm not a stupid kid."

"Sure, you're not. This stuff steadies me. I'm like a damn rock now." I noticed his slide wobbling all over the place. He laughed. "I don't think you believe me, James. I've got to concentrate to blow this horn. Don't laugh at me too much. How do my low notes sound?" Moses unlocked his slide and blew a few deep blasts. Wow! I have to say he played beautifully then. And loudly. I've no doubt he'd been fooling me earlier when he made strange toots and fumbled the slide.

"Gee-wiz! Better than me," I said, and I unlocked my slide, used my slide oil to lubricate things a bit and brought up the mouthpiece to my lips. It was futile to try to match him, but I went ahead and played something like what he had, note for note, with my best technique.

"Hey! Pretty good," said Moses, nodding when I finished. "Pretty damn good, son. You got some lungs there, James, is it?"

"James, yeah, that's right."

"We're gonna get along fine then, James. I get along good with the good players. I can see you're trying. Let's give the little kids a great show with some fun music, okay? Let's make this a fantastic circus for the kids. They deserve it."

"Sure."

"I remember some fine circuses when I was a tyke," said Moses. "I can still hear the music of those old bands in New York. The circus acts fascinated me. I could watch them all day. The men flying around in the air, the catches, the wire walkers. And the music. I loved the circus music and atmosphere. It was a place of fantasy for me. My home was grim. We didn't have much. Who am I kidding? We didn't have nothing. No toys to speak of. The circus big top was like a magical toy land. Hey, I think I might have seen a toy circus in a window in New York City."

"Yep, probably."

"I guess I loved circuses even then. Anyway I believe these kids deserve a good memory of the circus to carry with them all their lives. Everybody deserves one of those," Moses explained.

The crowd began to fill in when they opened the doors. The stadium seats crowded with eager and happy kids, jumping up and down, yanking their clothes and turning to the kid behind them to talk. Thousands of wild kids from the toughest homes in town, crippled kids, kids with burns and casts on their arms and legs. A lot of them were wearing the same bright red felt fezzes that I had on, showing elephants and tigers. I could see the kids that were orphans in a group, and some kids taken from their home just for the circus without their parents. The poorest, most desperate kids, had been brought by churches and schools and charities in big groups of happy gawking children, stepping eagerly down to their seats, with treats in their hands, hugging stuffed clowns and waving plastic elephants on the ends of sticks. Even the adults had freed their minds to think of the circus again. They were merrier and lighter in their step. It was the happiest crowd imaginable. I was surprised and pleased.

I looked around at the rest of the Shriners. A guy in front of me played the clarinet and he had one of those belts that were holding his pants up too high. Little wisps of gray hair stuck out from under his fez. Although Moses was ancient, he wasn't anywhere near the oldest in that band. The regular percussionists (they had a young guy like me with them) looked like they had been yanked out of their coffins. They barely moved their torsos or their long, skinny arms. I think one of them had a nose grown permanently to his chin. They were two dead white ghosts.

Until the conductor brought up his baton.

Then the whole band, every last shrunken corpse, came to life. I realized suddenly something pretty damn important about them. They all lived to play circus music.

And man, I'm telling you, they could really play.

"Welcome ladies and gentlemen, boys and girls, to our glittering galaxy of big top stars!" the ringmaster shouted as he trotted into the center ring in a red coat, glossy top hat, and high boots. The lights of the arena dimmed.

And those old guys, those ancient corpses? They were out of

sight, way-out wicked, on the first screamer to the last at end of the final show. And I could barely keep up.

CHAPTER SEVEN

And that was Gluey's little secret, but it took me a while to realize it. Gluey, it turned out, was absolutely nuts about being a Shriner. He had no interest whatsoever in classical music, although he'd once cared deeply about it. He'd been swept away by doing good, curing kids with burns, and cleft palates and cleft lips and orthopedic problems and taking those sick kids to the circus. He loved playing circus music for crippled kids more than anything else in the whole danged world and he wanted the Shriner performance at those circuses to be absolutely perfect. If he thought the tubas were weak, he wanted the sound to be better and he took it upon himself to use his own private pupils or, I heard later, even hire professional tuba players at his own expense to fill in. He used the teenagers that he gave lessons to as subs in the Shriner band and he wouldn't take no for an answer when it came to replacing Shriners. That was why he took his best young players in private lessons and recruited them for the Shriner band on the weekends. Also, that was also why he lived in such a teeny, lousy house with terrible old furniture and paint-by-number art of clowns and circus poodles, and it explains why he spent most of his extra money on the Shriners' circuses. Yeah, I found out gradually, from listening to conversations I overheard on the buses, that Gluey was funding circuses partially, the tent cost or the cost of buses or chaperones for the kids. He was dedicated to the idea of giving poor kids and crippled kids a day of groovy entertainment. He even went into Sonora and brought the damn kids across the border!

I wondered, when I found out what Gluey was doing, if his

wife approved of her husband's ideas, but I never did find out. Heck, I never even saw her or the kid! The circuses and parades meant so much to him that all his spare time was taken. He was busy every time I saw him. We barely spoke except for at lessons, and that was all business, too.

The Monday after this first two Saturday circuses I left a little late for school. My mind was still at the arena relishing all the fun I'd had there. And I'd even managed to read my Algebra book for a couple of hours after the first circus. Moses turned out to be good at not bugging people when they had to study. He liked to sit and drink. The other guys were mostly comatose or joking around. Then the second circus and the third one that night had been more fun than the first! I hadn't been so nervous. Shoot, the weekend had been a blast and I was enjoying the idea of myself as a real musician playing for a real circus. I'd thought it was going to be terrible being in the Shriners. I'd thought they were going to be a bunch of uptight Nixon-lovers. What I found was they were all about getting drunk and playing music and joking around. It was cool being at circus performances with them. I was freer at the circus that Saturday than I had felt in years at home or school. The fun I had with Moses and playing screamers with those old guys completely removed my memory of the other kids who didn't like me. I was part of an adult world, looking at kids as people who had to be entertained. I had this weird purpose that no one at school could guess. I think I've learned that the best secret to have in life, better than love for a girl or something you want to buy, is a secret charity which stays secret.

Most mornings I left early for school and walked around the desert so I wouldn't get attacked while I was stuck carrying my old man's heavy trombone. Those jerks who were after me in junior high were still after me, but they were never in the desert real early. And after school they didn't get out of the school fast, because they were busy slamming lockers on guys' heads, so I was safe if I shot out of class right away and flew straight across the desert. I lived on the other side of this big old piece of desert that was beside the high school. Creosote bushes covered most of the vacant lot, with a few mesquites on the banks of the arroyo, which is a dry river that ran diagonally across the lot. In order to get across the desert you had to go down in the arroyo. There was no bridge, unless you walked the far way around the desert to the north, which as I said, was my usual path. The bank of this arroyo in the middle of the desert was low on the path because kids had worn the dirt down in all the years they had crossed it and gone on to high school. In the morning I was always a little nervous when I went over the arroyo bridge on Fifth Street because that was where someone could come up behind me. I took a good look before I walked too close. I was glad I did it because twice I caught a glimpse of those jerks from rocketry and their friends and I crossed Fifth Street quickly to keep them from seeing me. Then at the top of the hill, I crossed back again with a big crowd.

Since I was late that Monday after the first circus, I took a dumb chance and walking through the desert lot rather than skirting the edge. I discovered to my sorrow that some of my old enemies still remembered me.

As I was hurrying across, carrying my old man's trombone, I also held one of those light blue cloth notebooks which I had decorated coolly with a large ballpoint drawing of Jimi Hendrix from an album cover. It had taken me a week to finish the drawing. I was really proud of the effect. Maybe I was admiring my drawing too much and that explains why I didn't see what was coming.

I'd gotten to the same place where I loved to play as a kid, imagining it to be a fort I was holding against the Apaches. All the kids played in that empty lot which supposedly was owned by Howard Hughes so we called it the Hughes' desert. I strolled down into the arroyo bed and was starting back out, when suddenly I heard the sound of people sliding down the arroyo bank behind me.

I spun around.

"Well, well, Jamesy, old boy," a voice was saying. Two blonde goons, like Tweedledee and Tweedledumb, with surfer boy blonde hair-dos dipping over one eye and cool-looking madras shirts, stepped down out of a dirt hole in the bank.

I knew them immediately. The two jerks. The ones from Rocketry who hadn't liked me in junior high. The pair of complete bozos who had bashed me on the head with rockets and tortured almost everybody at school.

I didn't wait to find out what the hell those jerks wanted. Of course, I can never know exactly what they had in mind for me. Maybe they wanted to invite me to smoke some dope with them or something, but I didn't stick around to find out. I wouldn't have wanted to smoke dope with them anyway.

I took off running as fast as I could in the direction of the school.

A bunch of lucky things happened. The fort in the bank of the arroyo was a little too far from where I was that day for them to get to me right away, and they hadn't seen me coming, probably because they were about to smoke marijuana. That gave me my first advantage. Secondly, they'd caught me off guard, but throughout the year I'd prepared myself for the possibility that they might attack, and I was ready to react. Thirdly, as they walked/slid down the embankment from this hole, they had to look down, luckily, because the dirt bank was kinda steep out of the old fort. Also, the bottom of the arroyo had broken glass. Their slow slide was another break I needed to outrun them.

I guess, they didn't expect me to take off running immediately. Although they were surprised, one of them chased me and got close enough, as I flung my bod up the bank of the arroyo, to manage to grab my shirt, but I tore myself away. I felt a button pop off in the process of getting myself free. Up and out of the arroyo, I ran blindly. More blindly than my usual blindness. I spun around to get away and saw the burning dawn sun fly across the sky like the old Greeks thinking it was a flaming chariot or something. I threw myself in the direction of the school with no thought of where I was running.

I could hear the two goons chasing me, fairly far behind me at this point, and they were beginning to fall back farther. I felt good but I didn't slow down a bit because I wanted to be well ahead by the time we reached the school in case some of their friends were within shouting distance of them. They might call out and get someone to grab me. I swung around to make sure they weren't getting to close, and I was pretty damn happy to see that they were fading.

Then, not looking where I was going, I bashed into something terrible.

When school had started up after the Christmas break that year, and kids were again walking across the desert to high school, a dead German shepherd dog, was found lying near the edge of one of the main paths. We all thought a motorcycle must have hit it. It didn't seem to have been shot and we doubted it could have been hit on the street and crawled into the center of that desert patch, which was, super large. But by this time the body had been out for a month and it was rotting something awful. The carcass was still there, and it was not a pretty sight.

I never once thought about where the dead dog was. I never saw it on the ground and had completely forgotten that it was near the path I was running on. With escape only on my mind, I ran blindly, right into the damn dead dog.

When I tripped on it, or maybe I should say plowed into it, I went forward, but managed to catch myself. The collision moved the dead dog corpse, wrapping it around my lower legs. I felt the ooze of rotten flesh and the disgusting smell of decay. I kicked to get it off my feet and lower legs, but though I was free, I had to deal with the filth and disgust I felt. I vomited my breakfast onto my new notebook which I flung into a creosote bush. I couldn't stop myself from vomiting though I tried. The two goons were still following me. By this time they were laughing and they watched me vomit and enjoyed that too. What a sick pair of cretins they were. And at least I didn't drop my trombone or fall face first into the dog or anything. I'm pretty coordinated in emergencies.

As I said, the two goons enjoyed watching me. They were shouting and laughing, pointing and giggling at my predicament. They couldn't have devised a better torture for me if they had thought for hours. Their faces dissolved with impish giggly pleasure. They were squinting their blue eyes with mirth, yeah, and falling against each other because they were laughing so hard. Damn, man, they could see my disgust which I guess, thinking the way their sick-o brains did, was better than any physical pain they could give me with their feet or fists.

"Look at him! Look!" Tweedledee said to Tweedledum.

I couldn't even take a chance to stop, but kept running for the school.

That day I spent wearing the delicious odor of dead dog as my cologne. And I had stains on my pants.

It was hard to walk home. I wanted to go back for my notebook, but I knew it was covered with barf. Lots of people at school knew what had happened to me. I saw the two goons leading some friends through the desert to see the dog now.

"Run into any dead dogs recently?" some grinning idiot asked in the afternoon. An in crowd moron, sheesh.

I managed to walk home with a big group of neighborhood kids, who knew nothing about what had happened to me, even talking about something completely different until I was home so I could keep my mind off of my humiliation. It wasn't easy to pretend it hadn't happened, but that was exactly what I did. I forgot about the horror as well as I could.

I carefully avoided my two enemies and never saw them again during that remaining high school year. I'm not sure they'll even remembered me my senior year, this year. I told my mother that I stepped in a dirty mud puddle and I washed my new bellbottoms out myself with the hose in a bucket and hung them on the clothesline out back of Parental Weirdsville, U.S.A., so she wouldn't ask about anything. Yeah, that's right, I got a new pair of Levi's that were wide legged. You really haven't lived until you've run into a dead dog on the first day that you wore your new bellbottoms to school.

CHAPTER EIGHT

Shortly after this, the extreme heat arrived, as it does each year in Arizona. It is a horrible time of year with almost no chance of rain or even clouds to block the endless sun, which beats down on you until it feels as though someone is gliding a burning torch about three inches from your skin. The heat coming off the asphalt knocks you out. The sun is so bright you can get a sorta blindness if you drive too far without sunglasses. The flesh of your arm scalds quickly on chrome parts of cars. If the wind blows, the moving palm trees sound like uncomfortable people trying to wipe sweat off them. And speaking of sweat, that stuff drips in rivers down the back of your legs, collects in the fold of your elbow and under your collar. Summer is a serious blistering business in Arizona and nobody marches around or has festivals or town celebrations unless it can be at night or at dawn. People don't want to pass out in the heat. Except for the screaming cicadas, things get quiet. Businesses shut sometimes for the whole month of June. The snow birds flee the state (and many of the Shriners were snow birds from cities in Minnesota and Wisconsin.) Plants wilt, people droop, and the circus and parade season in small town Arizona ends.

Gluey didn't call for me once in May. By June, I asked during a lesson whether he was going to need me, and he explained that my substitute trombonist job was over until late September. The Shriner parade business hadn't ended for the entire state; there were parades in Northern Arizona and the White Mountains, but that was too far for our chapter to travel. Gluey congratulated me on my performance at the local circus and urged me to continue lessons with him during the summer, something I no longer dreaded.

So the three performances at the local circus turned out to be the first and last Shriner events for me that school year. The circus performances with the Shriner band helped me some, because the memory of the funny old guys kept me cheerful. I was still surprised by how much I had enjoyed the day and looked forward to other events. I continued playing circus music with enthusiasm now, practicing my double and triple tonguing religiously.

By late July, Gluey informed me during a lesson that he would be losing one of his trombonists on and off all year, but luckily not my new friend Moses Grand. Although I thought Moses almost played well enough to cover for two members, Gluey wanted to keep the sound up. Gluey felt the band would not be up to its usual level of performance without a third trombone. Therefore, he thought he'd need me on several weekends that school year!

The fall and winter Shriner performances consisted of parades in rinky-dink Arizona towns, followed in the spring by circuses. For these events the Shriners travelled together by bus. On the third week of school, Gluey gave me the address of the local temple and told me to be there at seven sharp.

That morning I jumped happily out of our Plymouth, waving goodbye to Ginny and Mom, who'd driven me there.

"Step lively," called Ginny, being her usual pain in the ass. This was a dirty dig about the ox poop and my TV debut.

"Thanks, dork," I said, slamming the car door.

For the first bus trip, we journeyed to the small town of Crow Flats, Arizona for their annual Cuervo Loco Days parade. Cuervo Loco Days was the usual jolly festival of small town jerks fighting mock gun battles in the streets, imitating ladies of ill-repute, and dressing as outlaw gangs. I'd been to that idiot fest before. The Shriner band would play in the parade, riding on a float.

When I arrived, there was a line of ancient musicians

waiting to get on the bus, which was already idling in front of the temple. The Shriner temple was a one story brick place, kinda modern like an insurance agency or something, with lots of palm trees and pyrocanthus bushes dotted around. A fake arch of bricks in front of a phony antique carved door. One of those Mexican carved doors with squirrels chasing acorns.

I joined the back of the line at the moment when the driver lifted a silvery section of the side of the bus, the place where luggage usually went. Two old coots coming out of the temple greeted me as though they'd seen me the day before, and more ancients, hearing my name, came over to slap me (weakly) on the back. One by one the musicians fumbled their cases into this compartment, with Gluey helping since he was one of the younger members of the ancient band. Some of the old guys practically fell in themselves when they tried to fling their cases forward. The tuba players were especially taxed. When I got to the front, I slid my old man's trombone case in with all the other drum, trumpet, clarinet, and tuba cases. Then I boarded the bus. Two steps at a time.

"Wow," said Milton II, one of two trumpet players named Milton who was coming up behind me, "I forgot legs could do that."

"Here! James!" called Moses when he caught sight of me. He was holding a seat beside him for me near the back. Gluey must have told him I would be joining the band that day.

I fought my way through the crazy crowd of babbling old Shriners who were laughing and joking like a bunch of loony kids. A couple of them were trading mock punches and I pretended to duck. They all slapped me on the back again. Frank, the coronet player, wheezed at the effort.

"I'm almost perfect from the heart attack last month, James," he said.

"Okay," I replied. I felt my eyes popping a little bit at that remark.

Outfitted inside with big old cushiony seats and a toilet in back, what was different about the Shriner bus was all the liquor those crazy Shriners brought with them. Damn, lemme tell you, was there ever a lot of drinking on those buses. Whoa, I'm not lying when I say those Shriner guys were mostly all crocked. I don't know if this is some general thing with Shriners everywhere or if it was something peculiar to those Shriners of that temple or the temples in Arizona. Man, those jokers loved to get themselves boozed up. Somehow it never occurred to them that it might affect their playing, and if anything I suppose it kept them playing longer than they would have otherwise. The buses they hired were actually run as a rolling bars all the way to some stinking little Arizona berg in the middle of a dry and dusty hell.

They must have gone out and bought hundreds of dollars of booze for the trip. I suppose this was considered part of their expenses of travel. They brought in every kind of liquor imaginable: rye, scotch, vermouth, beer, wine, and vodka. I don't know the names of all the drinks they could mix. Sheesh, I'm not a damn drinker myself. Just imagine every damn weird concoction and you just about have it. The bar keeper would be different Shriner guys, but there were about three of them that did it, and the one you got depended on who was going along to play and who felt like putting out the effort to bartend. Not one of them cared about underage drinking. They were all for it! And how! I'm not sure I get their philosophy on that. They seemed to be very upright guys, very moralistic in general, but as far as alcohol went, they thought early drinking was dandy. I guess in part it was something of their era, having seen a little of Prohibition and not thinking it was any good at all, they decided any restrictions on drinking were stupid. The guys in fezzes liked their booze and they liked it non-stop and they weren't afraid to offer it to young kids like I was. They didn't worry. For a long time, and certainly that first day on the bus, I didn't touch a drop, but eventually I broke down.

Looking at it from their point of view, I suppose they thought they were getting young people involved in the act of charity. After all, they were helping kids with cleft palates and deformities and stuff, and if they got the younger people a little drunk on the way, that might be good for keeping them interested in the habit of good-deed-doing. They really liked it when young people were with them. So they figured if they were a little lenient on the booze they'd get young people to be happy to join. I even heard one of the old bartenders telling another young sub once that booze was better than marijuana. Booze is not exactly a healthy life-style or a good thing to be doing while trying to be charitable.

But as I was saying about that bus trip to Crow Flats, I swam up-current, against the ridiculous waves of drunken, jolly musicians who were returning to their seats with highballs and beers. When I got to where Moses sat, I dropped onto my seat beside him.

"How's it going?" I asked him. It was odd taking a seat beside Santa Claus, but Moses was just as reassuring and welcoming as before.

"It's going," said Moses with a shrug. "I never did hear—what did you think of playing in your first circus?"

That was probably a lie; I'm sure Gluey told him I'd liked the circus. "Oh, it was a blast. I dug it."

"Good, you have a taste for it." Moses nodded in approval. I noticed he was drinking an orange juice which I suspected was not without a large quantity of alcohol.

"Definitely fun," I said, still commenting on the circus. "I didn't think I would like it as much as I did."

"Are you ready for this adventure today?"

"Oh yeah. I'm stoked."

I looked out the window of the bus in time to see a dozen more Shriners stumbling out of the temple with drinks in hand. They boarded the bus and it actually got louder in there, which I would have thought impossible. Guys were screeching and screaming and slapping each other on the back. Then a few more men without drinks came out of the temple, followed by the driver, who closed the luggage compartment where our instruments were and bounded up the steps of the bus. He plopped into his seat and buckled his seat belt.

I found out that the Shriners liked to sit in sections on the bus, trombones together, percussionists in one area, clowns in another. Though Gluey was walking around the bus telling Shriners to be seated, the driver had a long wait before he could get going. Finally, everyone found a drink and a place and the bus crept forward. I noticed a truck following us out of the Shriner parking lot. This truck towed two of those dumb miniature cars in a converted trailer. They had lawn mower engines in them and were as obnoxious as all hell to have to listen to, but the kids always seemed to think they were funny.

We drove through town and out on the highway heading to Crow Flats, a dinky place in the middle of nowhere.

"How did you get started as a musician anyway?" I asked Moses once we were on the highway.

"Ah, well, James, my grandfather played the violin and he traveled with Roma musicians in Europe for many years. I heard these stories about his life. My father offered my older brother, Gil, to learn clarinet," Moses explained, "He learned it and I wanted to do everything that Gil did. So I began to play clarinet, also. And when he joined a Klezmer band—"

"A what?"

"Klezmer, you want to know about it?"

"Sure."

"Klezmer, it's a style. A way of playing, jazzy and fast with violins mostly and wooden blocks and cymbolines. Anyway it was popular in New Haven and I wanted to be in that band also. They didn't let me at first, but I kept up—"

"You bugged them a lot?"

"Oh, yes," said Moses laughing, "A lot of 'bugging.'"

"So eventually they needed another clarinet, which I could play a little, so I joined."

"Was it fun?"

"Oh yes. Very. I stayed out late and acted wild. I went all over the place with that band. We had a lot of adventures. We played for weddings and special events everywhere in New York. I got to travel and go to parties every week. These parties had the best food and good-looking girls. Oh boy, I liked it all right. What could be better?"

"I guess I could dig a bunch of good food. And pretty girls."

"Exactly. Then I liked jazz so I also tried learning a trombone. We added that to the band for the glissando. Another fellow came in for clarinet."

"Then why not play that now? Play in those bands that do Klezmer?"

"I still do sometimes, but when I got older I wanted to do something good for children. And when I had a car repair shop I became a Mason and went through all the levels to be a Shriner."

"I see"

"What nationality are you, James?"

"English and Pennsylvania Dutch, or something. I don't know what that is. 'Ach, don't be so shusneck!'"

"What was that? What just happened?" Moses spun around in his seat as though someone else had just spoken. He looked confused and beat his head as though he were attacked by devils, "What was that? Who spoke?"

I had to stop laughing at him before I could answer. "That means 'Oh, don't be so difficult,' so high handed, or something."

"That's Pennsylvania Dutch?"

"Yeah. It's the only thing I know how to say. It's like German or something."

"Good. I'm glad you can't say anything else. That was very strange. Don't do it again."

"Okay." I was laughing so hard my side was aching.

"Yes. A young person is better when they don't know too much about their nationality. Or about others. It's better if they keep an open mind. That way they make friends with everyone and see others as their friends."

"Okay," I agreed, still laughing at him.

"Yeah, I liked Klezmer, but I like any Freilech music."

"What's that--Freilech?"

"It means happy music. And I like to clown around."

"But you said you don't like the Shriner clowns?"

"No, they aren't even happy. One or two of them I have spoken to, that's all, in all these years. Clowns in general have a very interesting history and the good clown acts follow in classic patterns."

"Really?"

"Oh yes. What you're gonna see in good clown performances are three characters. There's the White Face who is dignified and he orders around the other clowns. And then there's an Auguste who has trouble or he's an anarchist. Then they add the Contrauguste and he tries to mediate between the White Face and Auguste."

"Kinda like an office feud or something?"

"Very good. That's the idea."

"You think these Shriner clowns aren't so good?"

"They are a grumbly bunch, James. Rather foul."

Moses was into drinking, as I mentioned. He always had a cocktail going while we were on the bus. Being Russian he liked his vodka, mostly, and took it with milk or orange juice. He took other liquor, too. It just depended on his mood. Sometimes he sent me back with a certain drink in mind and other times he told me to surprise him. He was quite fond of tequila and never objected to scotch. That's right, I was fetching all his drinks!

He drew a line at actually drinking on the floats during the parades. I suppose he thought that would be unseemly. None of them drank on the floats, but they drank everywhere else. Holy moly! The bus was completely free and some of the temples in the town we visited were probably set up like regular social drinking clubs, though this is just my idea of them, because I was never allowed inside, but the Shriners came out of the door with new drinks that they didn't go in with. Right before we left the bus for a float, Moses would take a last swig, one enormous gulp. He never spilled any on himself or me or his instrument. He was a careful, old Russian gentleman.

So that day, the whole band, except the driver, Gluey and I, had imbibed freely of the open bar as the bus barreled across the busy stretch of Interstate that led to the turnoff. The bartender set himself up at the rear of the bus, in a seat where he had all the booze and mixes in cardboard boxes beside him. He used old packing material to secure the bottles and had ice, plastic glasses and cocktail mixers. The happy crowd reminisced and joked and played tricks on each other as they rolled down the road. The fez of one of the trumpet Miltons, who was sitting in a seat a few rows behind Moses and me, was used as an ashtray by a standing Shriner. Milton I or II smiled happily out the window or into space as ashes filled the depression in his hat.

"Does alcohol affect your playing?" I asked Moses.

"Yes, it makes me better. Stronger and steadier," Moses claimed.

"Hmmm," I said.

The bus swayed on, leaving the Interstate after two hours. The big old thing hardly fit on some of the little roads that led into the back of beyond. I remember boulders and cactuses reaching out, scraping the sides of the bus. I read my Geometry book and I think I fell asleep for a while, because we'd left very early. We always had to be able to get to the town we were appearing at by noon or so, because the parades would usually start then. Nearly all of the parades that needed the Shriners were in little towns out in the middle of nowhere. Places that were good for gathering desert sand and misfits.

I don't remember the way down there, but I know at one point we turned and headed for a shallow red canyon. The grass grew in yellow mounds, big dry clumps. Off the main road, there were only dirt roads and many large ranches. At times the bus slowed to a crawl before we passed through a town. These little places were almost ghost towns with a small number of residents and boarded up saloons and mining crap left to rust in the Arizona sun. The activities of the countryside was now supporting towns which no longer had any mines in them. And there wasn't much activity in the countryside.

"These are the played-out places. Sad isn't it," said Moses, staring out the bus window, "All their wealth has passed on. To the East Coast, building bridges and millions of miles of copper wires and engine parts. Copper has been driving all the productive places of America. Now these folks are out in the middle of nowhere with nothing left to support them."

We passed collections of heavy rusted equipment, the bulk of an ancient America, giant gears and cogs to pull ore out of the rocky soil, ruined sheds where tons and tons of metal was yanked out of the dry earth.

"Look at the slag everywhere," said Moses, "like the devil's toenail clippings."

We passed melted masses of useless rock and minerals and red stained boulders bleeding rust. The equipment we saw everywhere was like giant insects, attached to the hide of earth and unwilling to let go, although the mining had long since ended.

"It's pretty lonely down here," Moses said.

"Yeah, pretty lonely. The little towns are a hopeless pile of crap," I said. Moses didn't care about cursing.

Two small towns we passed through were made up of the saddest collections of houses and the most pathetic ideas of progress you could imagine anywhere. And conservative, damn, there were signs about wanting no hippies. On screen doors, washroom windows, gates and garages.

I noticed Moses straining to read one of them. A few minutes later he spoke up.

"I have heard there is a nudist commune of hippies out here somewhere," he said suddenly with real interest, waving one hand around vaguely in the direction of the window beside me. "They say it's in a canyon near Mexico somewhere around here and there's almost a hundred people and goats living in it. In Geodesic domes."

"What are those? Domes?"

"Sort of space-age ball-shaped houses. Made of triangular pieces that you fit together. They look a little like igloos or nodules. Like a pimple with window panes."

"Wow. You don't say. And nudists are living in those? Girl nudists?"

"That's the rumor."

"I might wanna join them," I said, looking around to get an idea of where we were for future reference. "What's this place, anyway?"

"Santa Cruz County. Route 242."

"Damn, I gotta remember this." I had a stubby pencil and jotted that down on the endpapers of the Geometry book.

"Yes, that might be an educational place for you," said Moses, chuckling like some crazy imp.

"Highly. Highly educational," I agreed. "You don't know the directions? The exact canyon?"

"I'm afraid I don't, James. Well, I heard it was east of this road and before you get to Naco. But it's something for you to research."

"I'm a little afraid to come down here with my hair, not that it's that long—"

Moses agreed. "I don't think it's that long."

"Thanks, my parents hate it. I think my dad wants to sneak into my room at night and slice it all off! Some of the typical crew cut gang at school kinda look at me peculiarly. They cut their crew cuts flat at the top, so they're block heads. They always look like they want to shave my head the way they have it."

At one point the hillside beside the bus was studded with blooming agaves. "Look at those!" I exclaimed.

"Like a hill of artichoke plants," Moses replied, "but they're agave."

"Is this what they make tequila of?"

"I believe it's these or a near relative."

"Goddamn."

"They have whole farms of the stuff in Mexico. In Jalisco."

"Really?"

"Fields as far as you can see."

"Have you seen them?"

"Sure, I visited them once."

"I'd like to see that.... Moses, you're a very well-rounded person," I said.

"Thank you for noticing," Moses agreed.

Twenty miles from Crow Flat and the hills were smooth and rolled in beautiful wiggling patterns off to the horizon. It looked strange with rounded hills and these sticks poking into the sky from the agave plants scattered here and there. We went on for a few miles admiring these plants until they gradually disappeared.

When we turned off on the quieter stretches of mountainous road, a paved road which led to the rinky-dink town of Crow Flats, the crowd on the Shriner bus was that much more crocked and rowdy. Then, by chance, a Shriner named Ed, who played the tuba and always sat near the back of the bus with another tuba player, in the seat behind Moses and I, looked out the rear window of the bus at the stretch of highway behind us. Not expecting to see anything other than a rocky ledge that the highway department had sliced with dynamite and some scraggly patches of prickly pear, what he actually saw was a motorcycle with ape bars overtake and nearly cream a small truck.

"Hey," said Ed, after what he'd seen behind them had fully sunk in.

"Huh?" said the other man coming out of a daze and answering with a slushy voice. He had only mixed one Bloody Mary, but he didn't hold his liquor well, a fact his wife pounded into him every time she picked him up at the temple. "What's the ma-ma-ter?"

"There's a motorcycle and a sidecar doing crazy stuff back there."

Because of the rev of the engine of the bus going up the hill, he only heard some of the other man's words. "What stuff?"

"Just crazy stuff. It roared up and about killed somebody in a truck," he explained. "Back there at the rocky ledge."

Moses and I and some of the other Shriners overheard him and looked back to the spot where he pointed. I could barely see a motorcycle, a sidecar and hairy men. They looked like a couple of cartoon apes with white hair!

A small blue truck had pulled off the road and puffs of tan dust were floating away from the wheels of the truck as though it had been an emergency stop.

"It overtook the truck in a crazy way. The truck almost crashed. It's at the side of the road right now. Way back there," Ed explained and pointed.

"No kidding," said Milton II across the aisle. He held aloft a greenish highball in a plastic cocktail glass and it sloshed violently as the bus barreled upward. 'Madness, simply madness the way some people drive.'

"It's gaining on us," said Gluey. Gluey was usually the most alert of all the Shriners, because, as I said, besides me and the driver, he was sober.

"Hey, driver," called the director for the day, who had gotten word of what had happened. "Hey!"

There was no response from the driver.

"Tell the driver there is a crazy motorbike coming up behind us," the director told someone further up the aisle.

"What's that?" asked an excited man in an oversized shirt. "A crazy motorcyclist? You know what that means!"

A couple of the other old men turned around and stuck their heads over the top of their seats.

"Good God, those nutty Bastards are heading straight for us," said another when he had taken a look. "They're gonna overtake us in a few minutes."

"It's a foreign motorcycle. I think it's a—"

"What?"

"I believe it's a Morton ffuggles-worth Sapphire," said a drunken man who kept mashing his fez on his head with one hand as though a sudden wind might blow it off.

"There's no such thing," said Moses, "Are you actually nuts or something?"

Now it seemed Moses was an expert in English motorcycles!

"I know my English moto—"

"Yeah, it's an English damn thing, sure enough. Whoa, it's not slowing down a bit," his pop-eyed seatmate said. "A maniac and a sidecar."

"It'll slow down," a bored man concluded.

"Of course it's not slowing down. I think it happens to be speeding up," said a know-it-all with a cigar.

"It's gaining on us," screeched Ed, who had seen it first and was starting to hop around the bus with excitement. He had a hard time controlling himself whenever things got exciting.

"My god, I think it's two of those Bastard nuts!" said the other tuba player.

"What, they're not in this parade, are they?" exclaimed someone sitting ahead of our seat with real alarm.

"What bastards? What bastards are they talking about?" I asked Moses.

Moses responded with a start. "Of course! The Bastards! They must be here today!"

"I think so, Moses. Yeah, they said Bastards might be playing in this parade. What are they talking about?"

"By Bastards they mean the International Order of Old Bastards, James, also known as the I.O.O.B. I haven't told you about them yet. The Bastards are a gang of raggedy, smelly, obnoxious, obscene jokers who disrespect all that is honorable and good in the world, James. They're something to behold. A real piece of work. I don't like them, but they're awfully funny. Those damned guys are nut cases. If they're coming, you're in for a big show and maybe some trouble!"

"Trouble!?"

"They make a lot of trouble wherever they appear. They're a cursed bunch of hopped-up monkeys. We ignore them, but they're enemies of the mountain men. Oh, I hope they're both in this parade."

"Mountain Men?"

"Another band of kooks."

"Is this I.O.O.B. a band? A musical marching group?" I asked.

"Good god, no, James! How did you get that idea? The Bastards aren't musicians. I'd venture to say they don't know what music is! We play real instruments. We're musicians! The Bastards only know how to smash a bunch of dirty looking drums and toot a couple of sad, dented-up bugles. Those are the worst looking bugles you've ever seen, James, a pity to behold," Moses explained. "They don't even play instruments other than those, just bugles and drums. They're Bastards! Their name is what they are, James. Get me another drink! Pronto!"

"Sure! What do you want this time?" I asked.

"Oh, anything they're dishing out. Seeing the Bastards coming today has interested me."

"Okay, Moses!" I said.

I worked my way to the back of the bus. A crowd had formed near the back window. Everyone was still studying the motorcycle which was behind us, but approaching fast.

"Sure looks like that to me," said another man who took a look for the first time and sat down promptly. "I.O.O.B.!"

"Me too. I agree it's getting closer and closer at a faster speed every minute," added another.

"It's gonna pass us and crash!" screamed Ed. "A real crash in a few minutes! I'm serious guys!"

I got Moses a Bloody Mary. The bartender thought it was for me, because I told him to make it a little weak. No matter what he said, I figured drinking as much as Moses did couldn't be good for a guy as old as he was. I wobbled my way back up to our seats with the potion for my friend.

"Here you go," I said, handing him the tomato drink.

"That looks good," said Moses, dashing an enormous amount down at once. "I haven't had one of these in days."

The bus riders were still going wild over the approaching motorcycle.

"Nah, it'll slow before it gets to us. It's gotta do that." This was added by the bored man who was still piling his cigarette ashes into the hat of the Shriner who stared vacantly, and happily, ahead.

"I tell you it's gonna pass us and crash," warned Ed. "There's no stopping it. It's gonna come and come until it does the same thing to us!"

"It's getting mighty close," agreed another.

"God, that driver's a nut," said someone. "A nut of the first order. Look at the way they're accelerating."

"Yeah, a real nut case."

"Hey, driver! There a nutty driver coming up behind us!"

I noticed the driver nodding solemnly.

"Don't bother the driver. Let him do his work. There's nothing he can do now until the motorcycle gets to us," said Moses.

"Stop screaming!" someone screamed. "Everyone stop the screaming and let the driver think without having to hear screaming!"

"Whaddaya think we oughtta do?" asked a drunken Shriner leaning over the driver's shoulder.

"Sit down," said the irritated driver.

The drunken man who was lurching about at the driver's shoulder whirled around dramatically and addressed those of us in the back of the bus, "He is asking everyone to sit down." This drunk was now the only Shriner at the front of the bus who was still standing. Moses and I laughed.

"Why doesn't that motorcycle slow down?"

"Too big of a hurry to get to his own death."

"What can we do?"

"Brace yourself. That's all you can do."

"Yeah, get in your seats everybody and brace yourself," said another man who played the piccolo.

"Brace for impact!" shouted Milton II.

"Oh hell, it doesn't worry me'" said the smart aleck guy who was using the Shriner hat as an ashtray.

"Watch out!"

The guys ducked and scrunched down in their seats. Some pulled themselves into tight balls and others started crossing themselves and praying.

The motorcycle roared up to our bus and zoomed past at an incredible speed. The tail of it whipped back and forth as the crazy driver, whose jeans jacket bore the unmistakable emblem of the dreadful I.O.O.B., floored the gas and the cycle shot forward. As it passed the bus, the passenger in the sidecar lifted his middle finger triumphantly.

"He's giving us the bird!" screamed Ed.

A rusty, dented Dodge Matador, light blue with a white roof, followed the motorcycle and side car. It was filled with more I.O.O.B.s, who were also flipping us the bird!

Just then the bastard floored the motorcycle, plowing past us with a deep throaty vroom, rocketing down the road toward Cuervo Loco Days.

"Whoa!"

"I felt it go by!"

"There's a Bastard driving it. I recognized him," said a man in shock.

"Figures," said another.

"A crazy looking son of a gun. His eyes were purely buggy! Like this." A Shriner did a horrible imitation of the Bastard's face.

"Normal," commented another observer.

"Who does he think he is anyway?"

"Car! Car! Damn!"

I felt the bus yank to the right. Moses and I crashed shoulders.

"It's swerving at us!" cried Moses. He put his hand around me and had us duck.

"Are we heading off the pavement?" asked someone with fear, "That's really not advisable at a juncture like this."

"The shoulder is soft! What's happening?"

Our bus crashed across some cactus and small rocks.

"We'll flip the bus if we go out there!"

"Whoa! Hey driver, what do you think you're do...oo...ing?"

The frightened bus driver applied the brakes, too quickly.

The bored man who was standing and horribly drunk lurched forward, struck his head and fell to the floor in a crumbled heap.

"Help! Help him! Help!" someone nearby cried.

"We're back on the road!" screamed Ed.

"Thank god for that," said Milton I.

"I was never worried," Milton II replied.

"Those damned Bastards!" said Ed to me. "They practically killed one of us! Again! They won't stop until they have! They're as good as murderers."

A few minutes later, the man who was knocked out came to, didn't remember a damn thing that had happened to him, and we entered Crow Flats.

There we were—an entire busload of Shriners, bombed out of our heads, except for Gluey, the driver, and me. Our task was to get our instruments out of the bus and make the transfer to the float. I wasn't sure most of them could manage it.

I'd never ridden on a float before. I learned from Moses that the Shriners always used them. Given the age of the band members, this certainly was a wise move. None of them could have marched two blocks in a parade, especially since they all were smashed out of their gourds. To make them walk even one city block might have meant the death of several of them. Milton I and Milton II, for example.

The driver found the float on the teeny side street where it had been built. In someone's driveway, actually. As we pulled up, dogs were barking at us from dirt yards full of weeds and rusty cars. We got off the bus, and picked our instruments out of the bottom of the bus. I had to help Ed with his tuba. Some old ladies were drinking tea out of jars and laughing at the old men Shriners as they fell over trying to pick out their instruments. I felt rather humiliated by that and tried to help the two Miltons who were always in bad shape.

The float for our band that day was built over many weeks by the local Shriner temple. It was a clever thing, put together on an old flatbed that had been modified with some pipe rails for supports. A large chicken wire and paper mache crow perched on the front of the float, large enough to support two Shriners. The band had to use some made-up wooden steps to climb up on the float, and it took forever to get the drunken old coots up the steps. With the exception of Gluey and me, they could barely shuffle themselves forward. They carried their instruments very slowly and carefully; we left the cases in the luggage compartment of the bus. Once I got on the float I discovered there were small risers. I worried that the old drunken guys wouldn't lift their feet the four inches it took to get up those, but nobody fell. The bottom of the float had a drape of paper with the name of the local Shriner chapter and some words of boosterish crap about the town. The conductor stepped into a box made of plywood that came to his waist, so that he wouldn't fall off. And I remember our stands had tie-downs to the float. It seemed like some of the skinny guys should have been glued down or tied down in case the wind snatched them up and carried them away.

When the float was ready to go, several more neighbors stepped out from behind their screen doors and laughed at the big crow, whose flimsy wings were flapping peculiarly. A dog chased us and a cat in the limbs of a big tree in someone's yard swished its tail at us and meowed loudly. Maybe he noticed that weird gigantic crow.

The driver of the float was the man who built it, so he knew the ins and outs of the truck. We stopped at the local temple to pick up the Shriners who were supposed to ride on the crow, and they climbed on—slowly. Lord, they were crocked too! Although it wasn't too common, some little towns also provide a few member who could play instruments. At Crow Flats we got a percussionist who wasn't actually ancient.

Once the crow riders had settled themselves, the driver started the engine again and we drove toward the town's main drag. Each gingerbread wooden home we passed on that street had a stunted Chinaberry tree in a Bermuda lawn in front of it. The fat old trees looked like stubby men lined up for an inspection. I didn't think we were in very good shape.

As we waited for the parade to start, I quizzed Moses for more information about the Bastards.

"I think their name is a joke on ours, James. We're the A.A.O.M.S., right, and they're the I.O.O.B."

"Will they come after us?" I asked Moses.

"Oh no. Not at all. First thing is, we are on a float. Since the Shriners don't march, I don't think they can bother us. I don't think the I.O.O.B would stop a parade float. And they know we're harmless, James. After all, we don't ever raise a hand against them and most of us are not bothered by being called names or having the finger showed to us. We would never harass them or be offended by them. No, it's the Mountain Men that they want to get even with and they'll go after them. They have no fight with us."

"Who are these Mountain Men?"

"As I said, another group of nuts. They dress up as trappers. I guess they're not here today," said Moses.

"Don't you want to defend yourselves against the insults of the Bastards? You said they insult everyone. Like that guy on the motorcycle flipping us off?"

"No, James, nothing comes of nonsense like that. Nothing good, that is. We know it's better to be at peace with others. They're entitled to their opinions and the Mountain Men are entitled to beat the pulp out of them. The Masonic way is not to pick fights, but if a fight is going to happen between them and the Mountain Men, well, I will not be above enjoying it!" said Moses. "It's going to be very, very wonderful to watch!"

Moses kept looking for the Bastards for me during the wait for the parade to start.

Just when I was about to give up, he caught a glimpse!

"Look, behind the funeral parlor! Look there!"

At first I couldn't see what he was pointing at, and then I noticed some dirty men in a group. They had long scraggly beards and hair that was like blown weeds that had been swiped over and over on the oily undercarriage of a car. Maybe the best way to describe them is to say they resembled a gang of pirate cut-throats. Weather-beaten and grizzly gray pirates or evil Gabby Hayes look-a-likes. The old geezers fobbed along, swinging their arms and looking the part of the old western wanderers and bad guys. Some of the old chums looked like they'd been packed too long in cry-o-vac packages. Their faces had squeezed up features, pressed together. As they assembled, I'd never seen a more rag-tag group of gentlemen with dirty, saggy jeans, wrinkled skin and faded hopes. Their teeth were missing, stained, and crooked.

"These are some low-life characters if ever Arizona had produced them, James. Shoot, they are thoroughly rotten, a plague upon the parades in Southern Arizona." Moses chuckled when he said this, though. "No matter how much I hate them for their evilness individually, I must admit that their group is humorous. I don't take them seriously and neither does anyone else." The Shriners, Moses explained, had long since discovered the nature of the I.O.O.B. "They're idiots."

I only caught one more glimpse of the outrageous gang that day at Crow Flats. The glimpse I got was enough for me to know Moses was right. What a bunch they were!

It wasn't the way they looked that shocked me. It was their actions. They glowered at the crowd, laughed at children, kicked at dogs and marched out of step. The front group seemed to be mocking the famous fife and drum from Valley Forge. These gentlemen limped along and cursed the crowd. Most of the group was quite old, but they'd recruited some young men who probably were grimy miners from small towns who lived in trailers and needed excitement in their lives. They wore greasy-looking leather vests and had hideous hair. They were not the loudest, or the most obnoxious, but they probably were only learning their trade.

A quick end came to the Crow Flats' annual parade. Cowboys and wagons, carriages and bands, packed up and went home after showing what they could do. We were the best band in this parade, which was basically saying jack shit, because the others were terrible.

◆ ◆ ◆

"How did this I.O.O.B. form? Where did they come from?" I asked Moses later when we were on our way home in the bus.

"They formed out of an ether, James, out of the mysterious filament of nature from many unknown elements existing in the universe."

"What the hell?"

"I haven't the foggiest, James. Your guess is as good as mine. Those guys simply appeared in a parade a few years ago, and they've been coming to parades since. Who started the group? I don't really know. And what is their purpose? Frankly, I'm afraid to ask. What would happen to me, James, if I did? They're a rough bunch, that's for sure. To annoy people, maybe that's their purpose. But they don't annoy me very much at all."

I studied my Geometry book all the way back to town. Mom was sitting in the car ready to pick me up late in the afternoon when our bus returned.

Over the next months, I attended two more parades, which were similar to Crow Flats, except for no more English motorcycles racing beside us to flip us the bird and run us off the road. We saw the I.O.O.B. in neither of these parades. Then another summer arrived and the parade and circus season ended.

I thought about telling Mom that the busload of Shriners were always crocked, that there was a group called the

International Order of Old Bastards making fun of the Ancient Arabic Order of the Mystic Shrine and another group called the Mountain Men who hated the Bastards and that my friend Moses thought the two groups would battle, but what would she make of all of that madness and mayhem? Something bad, I figured. Frankly, I was beginning to enjoy my time with the Shriners and I didn't want it to end. Wow, it was out of sight to realize how my opinions had changed. Was I the same James who had been trying to get out of Shriner band with a lot of stupid lies?

CHAPTER NINE

On the first day of school that year, many other things had changed. It wasn't just the music or the clothing; the opposition to the war in Vietnam had strengthened among those of us who were young, even in backward old Arizona, and we'd convinced more of those who were older to march and protest.

On the second week of school, a student walked up to me near the end of the lunch hour. He stood before me, just staring into my damn face. It was so crazy. I thought it best to apologize quickly. The way I figured it, I'd probably violated some crazy school rule or something and I feared that I was about to be beaten up. This guy was big and he had to be a senior, because he had an impressive beard. Seniors had a bunch of dumb rules around the school, and one of their dip-shit rules was about this dumb plaque or shield set in the concrete of the senior patio. If you stepped on the school shield, you could be forced to clean it with a toothbrush by upperclassmen that grabbed you by your arms and pinned you down to do the scrubbing. Or so they warned everyone. I didn't think I'd even been in the senior patio in months, or I didn't remember going through there, at least, but I thought I might have been mistaken for someone else. I couldn't figure why else the guy was just standing in front of me, so I said, "If I stepped on the senior shield, I'm awful sorry."

However, this guy didn't budge or say a word and I was left trying to figure out why he was blocking my way. Finally, when he had studied my face enough, he spoke. "Don't worry, brother. Peace, man."

I realized then that he was not one of the usual school

idiots who would enforce a dumb rule like the school shield. He seemed to be different. Looking at his beard, I thought he was not the type to like any rules, probably. This was a new kind of kid.

Then I knew I was seeing at my school a real honest-to-goodness hippie up close.

He used a hand to brush his long brown hair back behind his ears. Then I realized a long ponytail hung at his back.

In slow motion he lifted a necklace of dark wooden beads carved into flowers from his neck and hung them on mine.

"Love, brother," he said, making the two-fingered peace sign and smiling.

"Yeah," I said sheepishly, looking around self-consciously to see if anyone was noticing the embarrassing thing that was happening to me.

When he left, I tore the love beads off of my neck and stuffed them in my pants pocket. I couldn't bring myself to throw them away. When I got home, I immediately gave them to Ginny, though I was rather proud I'd been given them.

"Did some **girl** give you these?" Ginny asked suspiciously. She seemed delighted with the idea.

"No, a girl didn't give me those. Everybody at school is going hippie. This guy came up and hung them around my neck today."

"A guy? That's weird. But maybe it's cool," said Ginny, in a second thought, uneasy with the idea that anything cool might have happened to me. "I like these beads."

Fashions had changed completely. All the girls who had wanted pale pink Villager shells, and Villager sweaters, and the cut-out Cappezio shoes were wearing flowered Mu-Mus. The conservative, well-pressed preppy kid look, had changed to Roman sandals and headbands. Everybody was flashing peace signs. They liked Jimi Hendrix, the Doors, and wanted to march in peace protests.

Ginny watched TV nonstop that summer; it was the boob tube or nothing. She started in the morning watching the toddler shows like *Captain Kangaroo*, and then she watched game shows, soap operas near noon, old movies at about two, and the local news before the national news. She sat there on the couch staring at anything that came on as though it were the most fascinating thing on earth. It was like she was retreating from reality. It really scared me. She wouldn't even walk up the alley to the swimming pool with me anymore. We used to walk up there and see how many sticker burrs we could get in our tennis shoes. One time the sole of mine was covered almost completely with sticker burrs from off the weeds.

I was afraid Ginny was becoming like my mother in the TV department and I told her that life did not exist in *My Three Sons* and *The Family Affair Show*. I kept running down TV all that summer, criticizing it and laughing at it evilly until she finally came around a bit and agreed that TV was not where it was at. She actually started listening to my rock records on the stereo and drawing pictures with me or making animals out of clay.

On Saturday nights for years our neighborhood association showed movies at the neighborhood pool. That September Mom told us she really wanted to go to *The Creature of the Black Lagoon,* because she wanted to see the male actor in it, not the creature, of course. Everyone went but my old man, who was real busy with his late-night work on engineering plans. We sat across the pool sucking on Pixie Sticks and watching the moon reflected on the pool water. You could see the palm tree fronds where they blocked out the twinkling stars. The monsoon rains were over, so there wasn't a cloud in the sky.

After the show, the neighborhood association gave out door prizes and Ginny won a container of Lincoln Logs, which those dumb wooden logs you can build miniature cabins with. I could see right away that she didn't want the toy. She was just too old, eleven that month, but she took the tube of them anyway. She was teary-eyed on the way home. All sorts of cars had parked on our street and the headlights were pulling away in all directions. Our shadows were big and leggy, moving places around us, travelling away in all directions. It was kinda weird but I could see that Ginny was proud that our street was somehow popular.

But she didn't like her prize.

"Be glad you got those Lincoln Logs," I told her.

"Why should I?" she asked.

"Just be glad!"

"I don't want to be glad. Don't tell me what to be."

"Well, you ought to be."

"I don't see why, Mr. Smarty-Pants." She was walking on the side of the curb. We had curbs that you could drive over to reach the gravel drives. They were like waves, and the gravel from front yards on the curbs was making her slip a little; she kept falling sideways which was making her more furious.

"Think about the poor kids in Vietnam," I suggested.

"What do they have to do with it?"

"They might step on bamboo with ox pee or poop on it and die of blood poisoning! That's what Ho Chi Min is doing to them." I'm not sure if I believed this, but a lot of people said it was true.

"One minute you're telling me to grow up and then another minute you're telling me to be glad I have Lincoln Logs!"

"Just be glad. Stay a kid for as long as you can, that's what I think." I told her this in absolute seriousness as it seemed to be my best advice to her. Doing the circus bit had made me think about how good I'd had it when I was a kid. Everything had been done to make me happy.

I was called again by Gluey a month later, in between lessons, and told the Shriners needed me that weekend. This time they were travelling to a circus which was being held outside a town on the border with Mexico.

That summer I'd learned to drive. My mom rode with me as my teacher and when I got to the parking lot of the Shriner Temple I got out and Mom did too, to take the car home.

I boarded the bus happily. By then I was beginning to crave more Shriner adventures, which had been really bitchin' and crazy so far. Who knew spending time with a bunch of drunken Methuselahs would be so boss. I was in a sleepy state when I reached the top of the steps and there was Moses, happy to see me and saving me the seat beside him again near the back of the bus. As usual he was already smashed, having visited the private bar inside the temple. Drinking at six a.m. Can you dig it?

"I saw you driving, James," said Moses.

"Oh, yeah, I'm doing that now. I gotta practice some more before I can think about taking the test."

"You nervous?"

"Ah, yeah."

"Time for another circus, huh?"

"Right on."

"Which do you think are better, James, parades or circuses?"

"Oh, I don't know. That parade with the Bastards was pretty crazy, man. I'm finding them both to be a blast."

"Wonderful."

"Where exactly are we going today, Moses?"

"To an old bullring. We've brought a circus there for the last three years. They don't use it for bullfighting much anymore. We're bringing buses up from Mexico. A lot of crippled kids are in little towns with no doctor and no circuses.

"Ah, that's nice," I said. I thought an abandoned bullring would make a good place to set up a Shriner circus tent, especially near the border. Moses told me that the Shriners rented the old bullring for a cheap price.

"The place is very old, though, James. A little scary."

That didn't sound too good, but I kept my trap closed. I wondered why we were always travelling south anyway. At first I thought it was because the chapters north of us were coming south to a lot of little towns and were more active than us. I think that was kinda true, but the real reason the Shriners went south was that Gluey wanted to do good deeds there and saw that the need was great for surgeries south of the border. He was always paying out of his own pocket for a bus to go across and pick up kids to see the circus. I found that out by listening when the musicians were talking. Sometimes he opened the snack bars for free and gave out toys, too.

On the way down to the bullring, Moses and I talked about many things. He especially wanted me to appreciate a funny bar where he used to take his grandkids when they were little. A long low building had this enormous cow head made of plaster on the roof. Like something from the Greeks, Moses said. A giant bullhead for sacrifice. Real authentic pagan Arizona cowboy junk. The building was a restaurant/bar with hand-lettered signs in the window. "No hippies, please." And "No shirts, no service." Across from this cow skull dump, there was a small lake with muddy edges and a few mesquite trees threatening to go swimming. I hate to say it, but I think Moses must have liked that place because the drinks were cheap. There wasn't much else that was nice about it.

We passed the old mission Tumacacori. Think of a filthy brown crumble cake. Shot full of holes and melting into the desert. It was the scene of a bunch of Indian rebellions and slaughters of priests. Moses told me about some of those battles.

And then we passed the high banks of Pena Blanca Lake. I told Moses about a time I'd been stung by a yellow jacket there. He was real interested in my memories. That's the way a good friend is, no matter what age they are.

When we reached the bullring, I discovered it looked like one of my great-grandmother's old teacups, chipped and cracked and stained. It had brown lines from water leaks streaming down the plaster of the Ionic columns that were stuck around the outside. It was a rinky-dink bullring, sad in almost every way. Some architect had tried to fix it up in the 1950s. That just made it more horrifying. Bullfighting wasn't very popular anymore. People were saying the bulls didn't have much of a chance against the bullfighters. So the ring wasn't used much, except for rock concerts. Mexican rock concerts were really weird. The fans probably wrecked the place more. The sewer was backed up most of the time. And any engineer would probably say the structure was unsound.

"This place is more of a dump than it was last year," said Moses when our bus parked in back.

"It's real shabby," I admitted.

"I hope it's safe for the kids," said Moses. "It looks like it's going to have a hard time not falling down today."

Moses and I walked forward with all the drunken Shriners. We wrestled our instruments out of the bus luggage compartment, taking our cases with us. I saw circus posters flopping in a steady wind. Leaflets blew in the parking lot. A gray canvas tent had been set up inside the center of the bullring. This big top could fit in, with the side panels stretched over the seats which left room for the animals to come out of the bull entrances and walk into the single circus ring. The top floor of the bullring had broken and boarded up windows all around the outside. As we went in, I looked up at these desolate windows, reflecting puffy white clouds across a bright blue sky.

"Look at all the broken windows," I said to Moses.

"Shoot, this place is a wreck. Hope we get a good crowd."

The once grand bullring really showed its age on the inside, too. The concrete seats were crumbling. The edges broken on the steps. Paint was peeling off the inside walls, the bullring sides which had been painted red.

"It's scarier inside," I said.

We found our band location, put up our own chairs and got out our instruments. We sat in the empty arena, practicing our merry music, hearing the canvas swaying and watching brilliant light flash at times through the openings in the canvas. It was about noon when we were in there. We all ate some hot dogs and drinks.

A strange sucking sound of the wind as it caught the canvas pulled on my brain like waves at the ocean. I thought my hair was lifting too. The inside of the canvas big top was gray and had odd stains on it as though it were plastered. The sections of canvas didn't meet, so slashes of light fell down onto the arena ground where the circus would be. Moses said the grinds went up row by row as though students would file in for a lecture. He also thought the whole thing reminded him of gladiators and the Coliseum, he said. Sounded right to me.

"Strange place, huh?" said Moses.

"You said it."

I'd never felt afraid of light before. When the big top moved it was like knives of fire shooting out. I hated the noise of the canvas ripping in the wind and the light stabbing where the audience would be sitting.

"The noise is frightening," Moses agreed.

I excused myself shortly after we played a few tunes. I needed to use the bathroom, which was really hard to find. I had to ask about six people for it and they weren't even sure. I was gonna give up, but I figured this might be my only chance until we got back on the bus. I found the whole arena to be scary and hated the idea of walking around alone.

It turned out the bathrooms were at the end of a long tunnel, a horrid gloomy tunnel with gory red walls and hideous, dirty cracks. This hall was like a bloody channel. It echoed strange hooting wind and the creaking noise of the canvas blowing above. Near the end of the passageway I found a door marked "hombres."

I can't explain what happened then, but I had a creepy feeling that somebody was already in there. I don't know how to describe it, but I knew that something terrible would happen to me if I went in. Someone was hiding in the closed stall or behind the door. Of that, I was certain. I didn't want to go in!

The instant I opened the door, I smelled something like a dirty swamp. One of the toilets had flooded the room. The mirrors were old and showed filthy walls. The light bulb was missing from the ceiling.

Without going farther, I shut the door quickly.

A second later, I wondered why I had done that. I was reconsidering my decision, when the urge to urinate was more than I could bear. Again I started to touch the doorknob, to go use the toilet, but I felt so strange and afraid that I stopped without going further.

Since I was a very little boy, I'd never deliberately urinated on a wall rather than go into a bathroom. But I went a ways toward the circus, down the red passage, and then the urge was too strong and I peed against the wall. I looked in all directions before I did it, and felt very guilty, but there was no way I was going into that dark bathroom.

I felt my hot pee leaving my body and watched it splash against the bloody red wall. I was finishing and about to zip up my fly when I thought I heard the sound of the bathroom door opening behind me. I couldn't stop urinating, because I was in mid-stream. I looked nervously in the direction of the bathroom and I began to flee, running a little crazily toward the arena, urine splashing on my shoes. Of course, I had opened the door myself, and heard the sound of it and that was what I heard behind me. I couldn't have been wrong. It meant that someone had been inside the bathroom after all.

Then I heard steps behind me in the long passageway. They were moving slowly, but gaining on me steadily. The steps wouldn't stop!

At first the blinding winter sunlight at the end of the tunnel made it impossible to see who was coming. I looked behind again, after thirty seconds or so, and then I saw the absurd figure of a clown: big shoes, false bald head, and twin gobs of flaming orange hair. A clown!

I tried to hurry up and get back to the band before the clown reached me, but he was gaining on me too fast.

He was right behind me, more quickly than I had realized, and he reached out and grabbed my collar!

My forward progress stopped. I fell against the tunnel wall and he was in front of me. He had me cornered.

"Hey!" I protested.

Freaky yellow eyes in a sad white face. Long yellow teeth. Strong hands with popping veins. This clown had strange, horrid eyes that glittered. I hadn't seen him before, but I hated him right away.

"Whaddaya think about the Shriners?" asked the hideous

clown. He poked my shoulder with the same hand that held a burning cigarette. I've always hated people when they did that. I didn't want the hot tip of the cigarette near my body, and I didn't want smoke in my eyes. I tried to pull away from him when he brought the cigarette close to me. But he wasn't going to let me get away. He put a hand on the other side of me and squeezed my arm. His grip was like a vise on me. I felt him enjoying my pain. He was squeezing my arm tighter and tighter by the second. I tried to pull away again.

"Huh?" I asked faintly and yet irritably. I wanted to get back in order to warm up with Moses and the band. This creepy clown was keeping me from getting ready.

"I have to practice with the band," I explained.

"How about growing up to be a clown?" he asked, returning to the subject.

"I'm just helping the band get filled out," I explained. "I don't want to join Shriners."

"You would like being a clown better than being in the band. We have a lot more fun. You look like you like having fun."

I couldn't imagine anyone who seemed to be having less fun than that creepy clown who was hurting me. I wondered what he was doing there anyway. Clown Alley was on the other side of the bullring. I'd seen the clowns go there as those of us in the band had been setting up.

"We need... some young blood," he said.

That might have been closer to the truth. No one wanted to join the clowns, but he might have meant something else. I had the unmistakable impression that he was dangerous. This was no happy clown wanting to recruit me to the Shriners. In fact I had the feeling that maybe he wasn't a Shriner, either.

"It's not my kind of thing," I said. "I don't like makeup and costumes." This was a lie, since I'd wanted to be in theater classes, but why not lie when you were being held against your will? I didn't owe this weird man the truth.

"Oh, whaddaya saying? You really don't like to make kids happy? A clown's job is to spread joy. You should be doing that," said the clown, pushing on me again with his cigarette hand. Shouldn't there be some kind of rule against clowns smoking in their costumes? It made them scarier than hell.

I heard footsteps approaching.

I turned my head toward the arena.

Just in time, Moses came up the hall, on his way to save me.

The clown narrowed his eyes at the skinny figure of Moses as though he were sizing him up to see if he could beat him up or something. I was scared shitless.

"You! Leave the boy alone," Moses hollered.

The clown pulled back with a start. "Hey, whatever..."

"What's going on? James, we need you back at the band. We'll be playing an opening in a few minutes," said Moses.

"I was trying to get back!" I glared at the creepy clown who dropped his hold on my arm, pretending to scratch his shoulder casually. He acted uninterested in me now, when he had been intense a moment before.

"Get out of here," said Moses to the clown who'd let go of my arm. Moses actually seemed to be shaking a bit, but I didn't think this was from drink. He was angry and maybe afraid, too. I'd never seen Moses in either of those moods.

"I was just talking to the boy about clowning."

"He said he doesn't want to be a clown. Leave him alone."

The clown strolled off. "Can't blame me for trying..." he complained weakly.

Moses watched him walk away.

"Are you all right?" he asked me finally.

"I don't know. I guess so. That guy really scared me. I remembered what you said about clowns. I was trying to get rid of him. He wouldn't let me go."

"Really!"

"Maybe we should tell someone. He shouldn't be in the Shriners."

We were hurrying back to the arena by then. We could hear the noise of the tent and see the sickening heights of the billowing canvas vault above. I felt ill.

"You know, I don't think he is a clown. I'm pretty sure he isn't one of ours. I don't know him," Moses said ominously, studying his retreating figure. "It's a good thing I came back here when I did. I think I'll call you my little lost one from now on."

Whether that clown planned to hurt me or not, I didn't know. But I was thankful that Moses thought to look for me.

Moses and I agreed that empty and derelict bullring gave off some kinda potent evil. But once the children came in, it was an entirely different place. It became gay and funny. The kids dashed down to their seats soon after the buses arrived.

Moses nudged me. "Here they come," he cried at the sight of them flowing out of the entrances all around the arena.

The tiny girls who came had little cardigan sweaters and dresses, black shoes (not patent leather, which American girls could afford) and pink, blue or green anklets. The boys had slacks and white shirts, their outfit for Mass, which, I guess, was their best clothes. Gluey had arranged to give the orphans fezzes, like the type I wore, made of red felt with tigers and elephants painted on them and the name of the local Shriner Temple. A circus was something special to them and I was catching the same fever that Moses and Gluey had. I never thought making a dumb kid happy would affect me that way. I guess I was surprised that there was so much I could do that would make another person happy.

Man, every kid there was wide-eyed with wonder. They had bused these kids in from lots of little towns in Sonora. Their smiles covered the bottom half of their faces. They pointed and screamed at the Shriner clown cars. Bags and boxes of hot dogs, popcorn and cotton candy covered their laps. Courtesy Gluey, probably. They eagerly filled the seats. They seemed to feel they had entered a shrine, had the worshipful faces of the crowd at Mass. The roof of the circus tent was a bit similar to the top of a Mexican cathedral. It had its billowing curves, was both convex and concave and was the color of gray plaster inside. I wasn't afraid of the light flashes anymore.

The conductor at the circus this time was a new gentleman and he wore Shriner regalia, a sash and a strange robe with glittery golden stars on it. At first glance he seemed to be nothing more than a merry man who enjoyed band conducting and had mischievous blue eyes above a large handlebar moustache. I was nervous about performing and after I met another trombone player that was a local Shriner, I mostly looked at my music and tried to practice a little. Then I noticed something a little off about the conductor.

As I mentioned before, I've never liked to stare at people and that day I really didn't want to stare at the conductor, so I tried to ignore what I thought seemed odd, but I kept studying him out of the corner of my eye to see what it was that bothered me. His head and face were normal; the fez the same as any other. His body was the right shape, but it suddenly struck me that the problem was down at the end of one of his arms. As I examined him in secret, I could see that he had a fake limb. Not the one he conducted with, of course, but the one that hung free at his side. It had a stiff thumb and the joined-together fingers of a fake arm.

"Moses," I yelped.

"Yeah, he has a fake arm, right?"

"Uh huh, but it's...."

It wasn't just a fake arm. It was much, much worse than that. This arm, I'm telling you, was like no other you've ever seen. It was the most wrong size fake arm that anyone could ever have ordered. For a grown man this thing was crazy. There's no other way to put it. The guy's arm looked like a doll arm had been hung on him. And it was the wrong color fake doll arm. It was like Crayola colored it from the worst flesh tone imaginable. A crazy person's idea of the look of normal flesh. And I don't think this fake arm was attached right or something, because it was too short. If you get the picture, there was about everything wrong with this arm that there could be. I don't think it was a question of them making this arm wrong or something. This man had deliberately picked an arm which made you aware instantly that it was fake.

I saw all this and swallowed hard. It was one of those things that you see and think "this is going to be a disaster." It wasn't that I thought he couldn't conduct, because obviously he could and I admired his style of conducting, however with an audience of kids, a fake arm, I say, a ridiculously fake arm that was like a doll arm, was simply tempting fate.

And it gradually dawned on us that the worshipful crowd of kids had changed into a big crazy crowd of lunatics that day.

"Shoot, this crowd is like the one on the banks of the river when David slew Goliath, James, and by that I mean it's getting rowdy," he said.

I was already rattled by the clown who'd harassed me. Now it was hard to see so many wild kids. I knew they were going to make a huge amount of noise when the circus started, so I was prepared to play loudly.

A bank of lights went out, which didn't change the arena much because we were outside, and we began with a rousing entry number, a Souza march followed by 'Entrance of the Gladiators'. A curtain parted and out bounded the announcer in a top hat and tails. He wore a large black moustache, which had obviously been pasted on his face, and spoke in Spanish, which was a good chance for me to not remember very much of what I'd learned. He made the standard circus announcement to ladies and gentlemen, boys and girls, in Spanish. As he spoke, he waved his arms around. Very few kids paid any attention to him. They were waiting for the show to begin. I was busy playing and could barely pay attention to what happened myself in the first minutes. Moses was right; I was having trouble with the noise and the audience.

Mostly the audience were school kids, but as I mentioned some of them were orphans who had been brought in big groups. Dang, a lot of these orphan kids were poorly managed when the circus started. They were tossing candied apples and pumpkin candy slices at each other like bombs and some of them were slugging each other and ripping clothes. There was a real skinny little kid sitting under a folding chair, and he stayed there through the whole circus.

The circus parade began and we really had to play and play hard. The clowns drove their cars in as a noisy mass. (I looked for but didn't see the clown who had bothered me!) Llamas strolled by in boredom and anger. The kids screamed and pointed at the clown cars and ponies and some noisy fuming motorcycles with brown bears riding them. Elephants strode by, holding each other's tails. Girl elephants had bows on their tails. Some trapeze people were riding the elephants and waving to the crowd of wild kids, who hadn't let up from throwing popcorn and stuff at each other and into their mouths. A set of fancy ponies trotted by, stepping in unison, with big pink feathered plumes on their heads. The ringmaster called for the kids to wave goodbye to the circus parade. The clowns did a crazy imitation parade.

The children kept their eyes up in the air for the next part of the circus. People on swings were flying, linking up with the arms and legs of their fellow artists and flying off together. We were playing along on one of the Souza things, when I noticed a little boy who seemed to be taking a special interest in the band. Moses noticed him, too.

"Watch that boy," Moses said.

"Oh yeah,' I responded. "What's he up to?"

After a while I noticed that he was coming right out of the audience, down some steps, and heading straight toward our conductor. What happened next was all in slow motion, like some bad nightmare taking place in a weird fishbowl. I suppose I sensed right away that the boy was heading in a beeline for the little fake, wrong-colored doll arm hanging at the conductor's side.

Well, I tried to be kind at first. The fact that he was heading for the conductor didn't have to mean anything bad. Maybe that kid wanted to get closer to the sound or maybe he was just going to dance around to the music. I thought he might be some sort of attention hog, the type of kid who wanted to take a big bow in front of an audience and get some applause.

"Somebody needs to stop him," Moses said, as he noticed what the boy was doing.

"I know. I think he's gonna do something awful to the arm."

"James, I believe you are correct, my lad, my little lost one," Moses said.

And yeah, I was right.

As I recall, he sort of oozed toward the conductor. He probably was with a group of orphan kids that we were playing for. No one had been paying a lot of attention to him. No one came after him to retrieve him. No one even noticed that he was gone, apparently, until the shout, probably from someone in the crowd.

"Hey, ay, carumba! Look at the boy! Watch out!"

Hey, they probably knew that kid all right.

The kid kept right on coming toward us.

He snuck right up to the conductor and he sorta smiled faintly for a while, a mysterious and evil smile, the most mischievous I'd seen in years. He had dark impish eyes, a thin body, and black hair, cut short to his skull. His shoes seemed too large for him, but they never fell off while I saw him. He held one of his little fingers on his mouth like he was contemplating whether he should do what he was about to do or not and he was looking straight at the little fake doll arm. And then he reached up. I knew something terrible was going to happen.

That was when he took the fake doll hand into his and after looking at it for a moment, he started shaking the fake arm in greeting. The boy had an enormous grin on his tiny face, he took the little hand in his and he shook it, all the time grinning and looking up at the conductor's face.

The conductor never stopped keeping time with his baton, but he seemed to be turning his upper body so that the fake arm would pull away from the boy. Also, he shooed the kid away with a movement of his knee, which didn't mess the band up too badly, but did nothing to stop the boy. The conductor's face showed the strain of the situation, even if his conducting didn't. He was obviously distressed. It was hard to watch. He couldn't pretend to be enjoying having his fake arm shaken like that.

I noticed that Moses had lost control and was giggling out of the side of his mouth, but his trombone was still playing quite well.

The conductor then went on without stopping. I suppose he thought the kid would get tired and go away. But this wasn't the type of kid to get tired easily. No sir. The conductor looked down momentarily. He didn't want to stop conducting, but he wanted to shake the kid off. He tried to step sideways and I suppose he hoped the arm would be pulled away from the kid, but the little boy held on, and stretched his arm as the band director stepped away. The conductor couldn't shake the kid off. Every time he tried to take back his arm, the kid managed to grab it back again. Pretty soon there was a real battle for the arm between the owner and the boy!

Eventually some adults who must have been the ones who brought him in a group realized that it was their charge who was up there creating a disturbance with the band.

"Porfirio. Come on. Back here. Porfirio. Porfirio, hijo!" a large woman began calling.

A man came out of the crowd. He was crouching and bowing and scraping to hide himself in his task of getting the kid out of there. By bending down, I suppose he thought fewer people in the audience would notice him, but in fact the opposite happened and more kids glanced away from the trapeze act to watch the bent-over nut who looked like he thought he was going to be struck. Then they noticed the funny boy shaking the conductor's fake arm.

The audience began laughing. Loudly.

Then a battle ensued to get little Porfirio, if that really was his name, away from the little fake arm, which he had taken quite a fancy to. He adored that arm. He wasn't going to leave it willingly. The conductor went on conducting though you knew he was feeling very irritated by having a boy run around and around and come back to tug on his arm.

Porfirio happened to be a wily little kid. Nobody could catch him. He was the kind of kid that in ancient times would have survived perfectly well in a cliff dwelling. I used to wonder how any of those kids in the cliff dwellings ever made it to adulthood without falling and breaking their skulls, and obviously some of them must have been made like this boy, wiry and agile as could be. This was the way they make little boys sometimes, strong and lean, wiggly and sneaky, and he could run extremely fast and dodge anyone trying to grab him and suddenly, lemme tell you, there were lots of people trying to grab him. It was the craziest, wildest scene ever imaginable with people running at him and him squirting away from them, under their arms, through their legs, around the bullring. He was the kind of imp who is fixated on his goal, a sort of one-track mind that returns again and again to the ridiculous desire of its heart. This kind of kid, wherever they exist in the world, could grow up to easily colonize the Moon or Mars or something, I mean he was a real survivor and intent on doing exactly what he wanted to do. You have to praise him for stick-to-it-ness. Parting the boy from the fake arm was not going to be easy. This was the type of person you ought to give complex and challenging tasks because they didn't understand the meaning of the word "no." They liked the word "no" for the opportunity it gave them to excel at determination. He could probably kill a whale or level Mt. Everest if he had that on his mind. What this odd little boy really wanted was to shake the fake hand of the conductor. God only knows why he wanted such an absurd thing. There was nothing on the earth that could stop him in his quest to do this. It helped that he was extremely skinny, intelligent and ruthless. There was nothing he wouldn't do, no chair he wouldn't knock over, no music stand too sacrosanct, and no shin that he wouldn't kick. The poor people who were attempting to stop him learned this to their chagrin.

"It's hopeless," Moses cried. "This is the funniest thing ever!"

"Why are they bothering? There's no stopping him!" I replied.

That kid just kept shaking the fake arm. He kept following

the conductor, persistently grasping and shaking his little hand. Boy, it was so funny!

"Oh, my gosh, he got away again!" Moses cried.

"There he goes. They can't catch him."

"He's off."

"That is the slickest kid."

"What, did he escape again?" Moses asked.

He ran around the back of us, behind the tubas.

"Please catch him!" shouted one of the men who were chasing him. I don't suppose he realized that the band members were older than sin. The tubas shook their heads. We couldn't stop playing long enough to try to stop him. Our band was overwhelmed by the crowd noise as it was.

"Here baby, come on," said one of the coaxers. The lady was leaning over with some food, maybe a hot dog or something, trying to tempt the kid away from the out-of-sight fake arm.

"Porfirio! Son!" shouted the doubled-over man, not pretending to be happy about what was happening. "Get over here and leave the band alone."

I could barely play; the whole thing was so crazy. Moses laughed so hard his old blue eyes were tearing. What a gas. The kid was crazy.

Moses and I somehow kept our eyes on the conductor and played our music and watched this crazy kid and all his antics and we laughed, too. The conductor was good; he never flinched, nor changed a bit of the music, but he didn't look exactly happy about what was happening.

"Oh! God!" said Moses once when the little boy was back at the fake hand shaking it and the music paused for a moment, "I can't believe this. It's too much, I'm going to burst! I'm laughing too hard to go on."

The pursuers began again by rushing him, but he led them in a wild chase around the conductor to the far side of the bullring and back all the way around the band. Some of the audience screamed to see what the little boy was doing. It was as good as a second ring of the circus!

"Will the party or parties who brought Porfirio Diaz please come to the music pit and retrieve him," said a droning announcement in Spanish, and then English.

But people who could control him didn't arrive. Or maybe he'd been brought in a large group without an adult who didn't really knew anything about him. Or maybe they were off buying beer, soda and hot dogs, with a whole bunch of other kids. I don't think there was anyone with him who he would have listened to anyway. He was too in love with the fake arm.

The attacker wore out the people who were trying to chase him. The conductor couldn't beat him off and continue conducting. Finally, the people chasing him got smarter and didn't leave the side of the conductor. That blocked off his access to his little arm.

When they dragged Porfirio away, he fought to get free. He looked wistfully back at the baby arm hanging at the conductor's side.

"Let me go back," he screamed.

"No, no, Porfirio, no," one of the ladies was saying shaking her head in disgust at what the boy had done. She looked as though she had glimpsed a foul part of human nature and was disillusioned forever.

Gluey and Moses and I were hysterical with laughing, but, eureka! The lessons had worked. During the whole thing, I was still playing.

I laughed and laughed, all the time playing the trombone as loudly as I could. Moses looked over at me approvingly. Gluey looked over at me approvingly. I guess I was playing all right while laughing, too, and it wasn't going to be the last time I laughed while I was with that band.

The woodwinds and other brass? Well, they also cracked up,

especially the clarinets, who really can never control themselves. But for them, laughing wrecked their tone and they had to stop or risk destroying our screamers.

But the trombone section? We laughed. We're the lucky ones in a band. The trombones can sneak a little gasping laugh out of the side of their mouth and still manage a decent note and good wind out of the big brass bell. Yeah, the trombones could laugh, and we did. You might find being able to laugh while playing an instrument nothing to brag at, or maybe not. I don't know where you're at in your life, man, but laughing is important to me. Not just in life in general, of course, but especially if you're ever in a band. And if you're in a Shiner band you are really going to need to laugh. The reason for this being that so much crazy crap happens around you whether you're on a stage or in a parade or at a circus playing the music. At least it did in the places around me last year. I don't think I was special or anything, so if you're open to it, a lot of crazy crap will probably happen to you.

CHAPTER TEN

How do you tell your parents about a kid trying to shake the phony arm of a band conductor? And is it even worth your while to tell them about a berserk clown that pins you against a wall? I, who was trapped in Parental Weirdsville, U.S.A., knew better than to try. Some things are best left unsaid.

When the call came for the next Shriner job, it was a parade in the town of Tough Cuss, Arizona and it was the highlight of my time with the Shriners.

It took about three hours to reach Tough Cuss by bus. Along the way we passed a country store, still operating, with a collection of wrecked cars and tractors behind it and a bunch of old harnesses hanging on the porch. The store windows showed piñatas and Mexican candy for sale, a sure sign that we were nearer the border. Past that store, lone cacti ran into dense patches, flowing into the smaller canyons, covering old rail lines, growing right to the edge of road cuts so that the roots hung out over our bus; they skittered along the roof when we drove underneath. We passed quiet horses grazing a field of weeds beneath a vulture sailing in the cloudless sky. At one point a mangy coyote stared with yellow eyes at our bus rolling toward the border.

That old town of Tough Cuss when we reached it had a main street called Tough It, a dirty street, rutted, unpaved and lined with bars and ice cream stores. The town had produced tons of silver and gold eighty years ago. Now it was played out. There was a large concrete ice cream cone on the sidewalk halfway down the street. Tough It Street was most of the parade route.

The driver that day was searching for the Shriner float which was supposed to be waiting for us on a side street near the town square.

"Mountain Men. Look!" cried Moses when we circled the square a second time. "Goddamn it, James, it finally happened. It happened." Moses pointed across the grass and the joy he felt showed all over the old guy. He became ridiculously gleeful. I followed his finger to a spot on a lawn under a small Arizona oak. "It's those goddamned Mountain Men."

"It sure is," piped up Ed from the seat behind us. "You're so lucky, James! This is gonna be great!"

"Sheesh, I finally get to see them," I replied, squinting to make out anything.

The Shriners, who were always loud, went ballistic as word travelled among them about the sighting of the Mountain Men. They were anticipating a battle between these Mountain Men and the Bastards, who'd paid the fee to be in the parade and probably would show up. Ed quivered with excitement and shouted to the two Miltons about it. Milton I complained that Ed was going to give him another heart attack.

I only caught glimpses of the Mountain Men from the window of the bus. From what I could see, the mass of men appeared to be some stupid Davy Crockett Convention or something. At first, there was this messy smear of yellowy brown interrupted by some fur poking out here and there. I realized, after I stared at it awhile, that it wasn't just a pile of old ripped-up suede and fur, but there were actual real dip-shits wearing complete dumb-o outfits of smoky yellow buckskin, rough side out. Every single one of them wore these goofy shirts and pants with long strands of fringe. It was the fringe that gave them the ripped-up appearance because every movement they made caused the slices to wiggle and jiggle. Fringe hung off their arms, on their cuffs, around the bibs of some pull-over shirt things, and even at their knees on one man. Some of them wore Indian-styled leggings, red and blue beaded, strapped to the back of their fat calves in a funny fashion. A lot of them had fur hats and fake rifles cradled in their arms like a baby or over their shoulders, casual style. Then I saw the jerkiest man ever, wearing a buzz cut, the suede suit, and a red, yellow and green striped blanket on his shoulders. With a blanket over him, he looked like he'd escaped from one of those kidnap breakfasts that girl in Algebra was so crazy about.

"There'll be a battle," said Moses cheerfully, "if the I.O.O.B. are here. And they're supposed to be. The Mountain Men are sworn enemies of the Bastards. I tell you, James, the Mountain Men are just about as pompous a group of old men as the Bastards are wild. The Mountain Men take themselves and their mission in life very seriously. They're concerned with how authentic they can make their costumes down to the smallest aspect like the buttons being made of real horn. It's total madness, of course. They detest the sloppy Bastards and have actually gone so far as to try to have them removed from parades. This has not been lost on the I.O.O. B. and true to their reputation, the Bastards vow to do dirt to the Mountain Men. There's bound to be big trouble."

In wanting to see a fight, Moses wasn't alone. All the Shriners were gleeful about the upcoming clash for the sheer entertainment value. Both groups were full of Divas and most of the members were mad out of their gourds, as Moses liked to say. The mere sight of the Mountain Men, knowing that they would be in a parade, made all the other Shriners take to drink stronger than ever. And loud? They were shrieking with excitement. They wanted to enjoy themselves and get set to relish the upcoming battle between the Bastards and the Mountain Men. Every man knew there was going to be a battle, as sure as Custer's men knew they were in trouble, and Moses said he wanted to be good and prepared for "the showdown," as he called it. I was not convinced that anything would happen.

Our bus pulled up next to the float and near the Mountain Men.

"There's Mr. Thom," cried Moses, who was craning backwards to see.

"Who?" I asked.

He pointed toward a crabby-looking man. "The skinny guy with the red face and the blue beads on his purse. He's a sour man, as nasty as any of the Bastards, except they don't know it yet. Mr. Thom doesn't like anyone making fun of them or the old west. I know there'll be a fight if the I.O.O.B. and Mr. Thomp are together in the same parade. They'll tear each other to bits!"

"Shoot, Moses, who are you going to root for? The Mountain Men or the Bastards?" I asked.

"Ah, very good question, James. I'll have to think about it for a while. But I don't care for either of them, so," Moses considered, "given that they're both blithering idiots, let's root for general chaos, shall we?"

I knew what chaos meant and it sounded fun to me. "Groovy!"

"Groovy."

"Listen, little lost one," Moses asked, "fetch me another drink. If we have the Bastards together with the Mountain Men I need to be thoroughly drunk. I've been wanting this to happen for five years!"

I got him a drink, watered-down, of course. I suppose Moses noticed, but he didn't complain.

"Is it wrong to root for them to go after each other?" he asked when I handed him a vodka and tonic.

"Yeah," I said.

"Yes, it probably is wrong. I can't stop myself," said Moses with a shrug. He downed about half the drink in one gulp. This was his usual procedure.

"Human nature," I agreed.

"That's right. I could pretend I wanted to stop it."

"Honesty is better."

"Sure. It is always best to be honest about your failings. Especially with yourself."

When we got off the bus, collected our instruments, and mounted the float, I got a better look at the Mountain Men. They were meticulously costumed, except for their odd haircuts. These gentlemen were so opposed to being taken for hippies that almost all of them had shaved their hair into crew cuts.

They stood calmly and chatted. Some had red target-like circles, Indian rosettes, which were beaded on their shirts. Their flies buttoned with a triangular flap. Eagle or turkey feathers poked from their hats, proudly perking into the turquoise sky. They had a lot of stone pipes, tobacco pouches, and purses strung around their necks. They all wore moccasins.

"I've heard the Bastards say terribly things about the crowds at parades and the dignitaries," said Moses, "and even their own mothers. Imagine, most people say bad things about other peoples' mothers."

Cue the Bastards. Moses had no more than said this, when they arrived.

Whacking their drums in no particular rhythm, they took the town square. Of course the group of Bastards were a complete contrast to the Mountain Men. They stomped through the town square, hollering and whooping, screaming and cursing. The Bastards rolled their eyes around and blew their foul breath into bugles. According to Moses, they had no respect for the towns they were in and liked to litter and pee at the back of shops. They made sport of the names and famous places in the little towns they marched in, and they shuffled and staggered around, imitating the brave men of Valley Forge with their own dirty drum brigade.

One Bastard led a sad looking donkey into their ranks.

"There will be bad blood between the Mountain Men and the Bastards, mark my words," Moses predicted. "And that donkey bites."

I sorta spaced out before the parade that morning, but when the announcer's melodious baritone boomed from the speakers hidden in the rafters of Tough Cuss' covered sidewalks, I woke up.

"Welcome, ladies and gentlemen, to the 56th annual Tough Cuss Parade," said the loudspeakers. Everywhere people froze and looked around. "And to begin our parade," the voice continued, "we welcome our Kiwanis from Tough Cuss. Let's hear it for the Kiwanis! Today they will be riding matched palomino ponies from Los Guapos Ranch..."

Horror of horrors. There in front of me the Kiwanis, dressed in tight spangled blue coats on palomino ponies with a banner held between them, spurred their ponies onto the parade route. The little horses whinnied and tossed their manes.

"Those poor ponies," said Moses, grinning at the bouncing bottoms of a couple of large Kiwanis as the ponies trotting away. With the strain on the ponies obvious, the crowd smiled and a few laughed. Moses and I chuckled.

A gang of girls, best friends I guess, strolled toward the town post office, which was across the corner from our staging center. For a while I could only catch quick glimpses of them through a hedge of cactus, and I'm kinda blind, but even in blurry glimpses I could tell they were awfully pretty girls and all of them were decked out in white dresses, those short, Mexican-style peasant dresses with embroidery near the neck. Only one of them actually looked like she might have been Mexican, and she was the prettiest. I couldn't stop watching them when they gathered around a gift shop window next to the post office. I think they were looking at a display of turquoise earrings that I had noticed earlier.

Suddenly, one of the bastards spied them, too.

"Here I am, girls! Girlies! Oh Girls! Kissy, kissy! Come and get me!" called this Bastard, and he was the ugliest member of the I.O.O.B.—if one could be said to be uglier in that gross group. He turned around and he had a raw section of bare pink skin above his slouchy bellbottom jeans. He shook his disgusting rear end in a provocative fashion at the girls and then spun around quickly and charged toward them, running in an idiotic fashion, which caused them to scream and scatter around the corner of the post office in the direction of the police station. "Where are you going, girls!?" he bellowed.

This creep strolled happily back to his gang after frightening the girls. The Bastards were laughing heartily, slapping the harasser on the back.

"Sir, I saw what you did. That was incredibly rude. Have you no shame?" asked a Mountain Man loudly as he stepped up to the teasing Bastard. As the Mountain Man spoke, his wolf pelt cap bobbed furiously. Righteous fury, that's what he was dealing out to the Bastard. In a voice that quavered with anger and insult.

"Here we go," whispered Moses to me as he watched this latest development and he winked at several Shriners on the float with us who had also heard the whole thing. "The fiasco begins. The opening chapter of their battle. It's like the Trojans and the Greeks. Without ships."

"Yeah, Moses, this is it!" said Ed blinking happily with his tuba on his lap behind me. "A pimple on any butt will eventually come to a head."

"Is that supposed to be profound?" asked the baritone.

"Works for me," said the other tuba.

"What an assortment of losers," called Mr. Thom loudly in the direction of the Bastards. He had real scorn in his thin, reedy voice. "How could there be a group of people more apt to run down the whole concept of what it means to be human." Mr. Thom was joined by one huge man with a barrel chest and a red face. Fringe hung from his shoulders, sleeves, and outlined his pockets.

"Ooohhh, ooohhh, did we make the itil bitl raggedy rawhidey boys angwy," said the Bastard right back, smiling with a mouth full of hideous teeth at Mr. Thom. To harass and taunt young women and the Mountain Men, especially Mr. Thom, seemed to make the I.O.O.B. happiest, according to what Moses whispered to me. The other Bastards were positively beaming.

"You are a shame to our nation and this parade," chimed in the man wearing the wolf pelt.

"Waaaaaa, de waaa waa," said one of the bastards in

response.

"Oh, this is going well," Moses said.

"Why, you could be a group of tramps on the street corner," said Mr. Thom scornfully, "A band? Pooh! What are you playing? Can anyone tell? Can you even carry a tune?"

Several of the Bastards noticed us, the Shriner band, intently watching the confrontation. All the old band members were leaning toward the argument with smiles on their faces. Of course, they were all crocked as well as happy.

"Hey, coneheads, what are you laughing at," a Bastard shouted at us.

"Moses!" I said.

"What's in your little hats?" asked the I.O.O.B. man.

This Bastard worried me. "Moses!"

"Don't worry, James. Don't fret so much. The trouble will be between them, not between us and them."

"Oooohhh, I'm a Mountain Man and I'm upset by all the baddie guys. Ooooohhh...boo fucking hoo..." The original jackass who was saying this pretended to cry, rubbing his eyes with his fists and wiggling his bottom again.

Just then the parade announcer spoke: "Ladies and Gentlemen," he said, "today we welcome Southern Arizona's most unique organization: The International Order of (Dare I Say It Aloud) Old Bastards!"

The Bastard who had just insulted the Mountain Men gave the one finger salute. He spun around in a zany fashion, and all the wild geezers assembled themselves, if you could call what they did assembling, and poured down the street like a foul flood. The awful expanse of their group looked like the contents of a pack rat nest.

"Some people think it's funny to make fun of the past," said one of the Mountain Men loudly, "I wouldn't venture an opinion about the lack of humanity, though. They certainly don't appear to be human. I can't understand how they are allowed in any parades." He was watching the International Order of Old Bastards wambling away.

"Hey, man, uptight anyone?" This was directed at the Mountain Men by another Bastard who stumbled after his group.

"Got some problems, buddies? Problems with the way we look?" A remaining Bastard who said this walked close to Mr. Thom's crabby face.

"I could look better than you men in my pajamas after a tornado. I think some of you are wearing pajamas!" proclaimed Mr. Thom.

"Well, toodly-poodly to you!" said the Bastard.

"Wow!" said Moses watching with real interest. "It's brewing up nicely! This is going to be very interesting in a few minutes, I predict."

"Next, Ladies and Gentlemen, the town of Tough Cuss is proud to welcome one of the best dressed groups in Southern Arizona: The Mountain Men!'

"Oh no," I cried, "They're going to be marching beside each other! They're in the parade one after the other!"

"Goddamn!" exclaimed Ed happily, slapping his knee. "What luck!"

"Oh yes! It has never happened before. This is a disaster!" exclaimed Moses joyfully. Moses rose so he could see everything, "I have waited so long for this day!"

"Moses! We're about to go! Sit down!" I said, yanking on his Shriner outfit. I didn't want to think of him falling off the float. Moses reluctantly sat down after complaining that I was nothing but an annoying old mother hen.

One by one the marching Mountain Men hiked their flintlock rifles on their shoulders and with everything copasetic in their step, joined together as a huge suede-skinned beast to display themselves in the parade.

"Ladies and gentlemen, our next parade entry is the Shriners band from the Habbar Temple!"

"We get to go right behind them. We'll be able to see everything," Moses said. I think he rubbed his hands together. He was like a kid who finds out he's getting a puppy for

Christmas. Within a few seconds, our float jerked forward and we were following the parade route!

◆ ◆ ◆

Our driver hung a left at Peanuckle Street, which led to Tough It. We continued playing as usual, but every Shriner looked ahead for what we would see on the parade route. Now we felt certain there was going to be a battle, and we were just waiting to come upon it.

And we weren't disappointed.

"Oh god!" yelled a woman, running around the corner on a sidewalk.

"Oh Zeus, please let this battle begin," shouted Ed, being ridiculous.

The scene that greeted us upon turning on Tough It Street was truly spectacular and horrifying. People battled everywhere. It was pandemonium. Utter and complete pandemonium, man. The two groups had only managed to march a few blocks before the hatred they felt had boiled over and they began attacking each other. Blows were flying in every direction I looked. It was as though the whole street was a boxing ring.

The driver of the truck that was towing us came to an immediate halt rather than run over anyone, which caused the old Shriner guys around me to spill forward. Instruments flew out of our mouths, eyes popped, unsecured sheet music abruptly soared in different directions. I tried to catch a few sheets. Only the ancient percussionists carried on. The band director turned to see what had caused the sudden stop and his eyes nearly popped out of his head.

It was quite a tableau, a feast for the eyes. In every direction Bastards had hold of Mountain Men and vice versa. There were punches flying and men being kicked, hair pulled, hats thrown away, fringe ripped (the Mountain Men, obviously, were suffering the worst in this respect) and beards being yanked. (The I.O.O.B had filthy beards and nothing would have convinced me to put my hands near their foul hair.) It was a vast melee, a huge battle of men versus men on sidewalks, in the street, and up alleys.

The first thing that I saw that I could describe was a Bastard dragging a Mountain Man beside him, screwing his knobby hand into the Mountain Man's hair and clouting him on the head with a banged-up bugle several times as they wrestled in front of a dentist's office. Up steps, pounding, running from a Mountain Man, another Bastard on the sidewalk yelped. The crowd of parade watchers fell away in horror.

"Oh my," said Moses. "Here it comes!"

"This is most distressing," said Gluey, the only Shriner who seemed upset by the fighting.

"Look over there," I cried. I'd seen a bigger battle in the center of the street which raged like a barroom brawl. Fists were flying wildly. The Bastards seemed to have the upper hand, with the exception of Mr. Thom who was as mean as his personality in battle.

"Gee, this is incredible," said Moses, enjoying the fierce fighting which raged all around us. By now we'd all stopped playing music. Our eyes traveled over the scene.

A Mountain Man was yanking the beard of a Bastard soundly and whisked away the kerchief from his head. Another Bastard crept up to the original Mountain Man and grabbed a buckskin pouch in both hands. He pulled the pouch in a downward motion. Very soundly. There was a horrid ripping sound when the pouch came free and it was tossed toward a town garbage can.

"Oww! Get off," the disrespected Mountain Man tried to clobber the Bastard with his rifle. "I've never been attacked like this. Police!"

After this success, the Bastard lurched off the curb, stepped down to the street, and fell upon the next Mountain Man he saw, seizing his wide sideburns and smacking his hat so quickly that it sailed off his amazed head.

"Glor...," he didn't get another peep out, for the Bastard grabbed his beard and tugged.

"Ahhhh!" screamed the man.

"No, not you. I want him," roared this Bastard, intent on grabbing Mr. Thom. The snide leader of the Mountain Men was battling several vicious Bastards simultaneously. Somehow the donkey had gotten in between them. It was biting Mr. Thom's arm.

Another old coot of a Mountain Man stumbled up the wooden steps to the boardwalk, but not before one of the I.O.O.B. with long fingers snatched at his layers and layers of long dangling suede fringe on his arms. "Mister, you're plumb crazy!" shouted the Mountain Man.

"Convenient stuff," the Bastard shouted back, reeling the puzzled man in.

"Hey, hey, how's he? Pulling me? Stop that, sir, you're ruining my costu—ack!"

A wheezy man, watching the whole thing, doubled over laughing and got kicked in the shins.

The crowd screamed even louder and began running, and the people who weren't screaming clung to posts along the covered sidewalk and gawked at the scene. One of the Bastards had his grubby hands around the fringe of a Mountain Man and was tearing fringe away right and left. On the Bastard's face there was a peculiar faraway look, totally disregarding the helpless man in her hands, though not releasing him.

"Here come the police cars," said Moses when we heard two sirens.

The squad cars pulled up on a side street and four officers scrambled out.

About the time the police arrived, Mr. Thom could be seen pinching the material of a Bastard's grimy yellow bandana. He succeeded in yanking it off the Bastard's head, and tossed it to the screeching crowd. With the Bastard squealing like a stuck pig, Mr. Thomson reached his scrawny fingers onto the Bastard's head and mussed his hair violently.

"Get these wild men out of here," a lady screamed at the police.

A spry gentleman, scampered away from the battle. "You won't get your evil claws on me, you friend of the devil, you fiendish hell hag!" He was yelling at a Bastard.

'Not so fast!' shouted a big Bastard. "Let me see about you!"

Before the escapee could protest, the big Bastard had his knobby hand intertwined in the long, scraggly, grizzly gray beard. He worked his skinny fingers around the gray hair, tightening his grip and then with a tremendous tug yanked down soundly. The crowd shrieked when the old gent's eyes bugged and his tongue popped out.

When his beard proved real, the big Bastard instantly lost interest in him and shot his bony leg out and tripped another escaping mass of rawhide. The Bastard snatched the wolf head off the escaping man and brandishing the floppy furry pelt swiped around in the air, feeling for another victim who might be trying to escape him. He held back another escapee with the iron grip of an arm and said, "Oh, where do you think you're going?"

Then groping his way through the crowd of old coots he ripped and tore at their hair and beards probing for weakness among this strange shredded variety of human kind.

"You leave us alone!" shouted a skinny man who looked like a package of old meat that had fallen out of a freezer.

The donkey stopped in place when the old man said this and it looked around rather sleepily.

A large police officer stepped off the boardwalk directly in front of Mr. Thom. At that point in the fight Mr. Thom seemed to be a major perpetrator of the battle as he had several Bastards in his grip and was thrashing them.

"Break it up," shouted the officer to Mr. Thom, "I am now placing you under arrest for disorderly conduct. I am requesting that you step out of the street. You're obstructing the progress of the parade."

"Police!" shrieked Mr. Thom when he realized the three Bastards now had hold of him.

Somehow, and boy, it was weird to watch, Mr. Thom shook himself free of the Bastards, but his mistake was to fall upon the policeman, touching his person, something which even I knew you never did with an officer.

"I have to advise you that you are touching an officer of the law..." said the policeman calmly.

"I have a job for you, officer. I want you to get this damn biting donkey out of my way."

"Sir, I am advising you—"

"Get—!"

This police man didn't wait for Mr. Thom to finish. Instead he escorted him, actually yanked him, up a side street to one of the waiting patrol cars where he intended to complete the formalities necessary to take Mr. Thom into custody. Mr. Thom's authentic moccasins slipped and lurched on the wooden plank sidewalks of the old mining town. He cursed wildly at the idea of being arrested, something that was well overdue for all of them.

"The street is clear. Now get this float going, now!" yelled another policeman at our driver. "Get out of here. You're holding up the whole parade!"

Policemen were breaking up fights all around us.

"Okay, sir!" said our driver nervously.

We braced ourselves as best we could and the driver accelerated.

As we pulled away, I noticed the scattered Mountain Men and Bastards standing about in disarray. The decimated ranks of both groups stood motionless in the street, the look on the face of the driver of our float was one of sheer terror as he drove right through the confused fighters, narrowly missing many of the Gabby Hayes look-a-likes who sprang away with surprising swiftness. Some of them ripped their pants in the process, or dropped their coonskin caps as they scampered in lively fashions to safety at the side of the street. It was as though the movie set of a western had exploded with silly characters.

I joined in on the Souza march we were playing, but I managed to see one last funny scene.

It was unmistakable. The figure of Mr. Thom scuffled away in the direction our float was going. He'd escaped arrest, but a policeman was giving chase!

Outside the Ye Olde Times Rock Candy and Novelty Gift Boutique, Mr. Thom panicked. When he saw the enormous plaster ice cream cone with a pink painted ball of ice cream and a brown waffle cone, he managed to scurry behind it, and he wedged himself in the space between the cone and the wall of the ice cream store. Who knows what he was thinking.

The officer tried to pull him forward and he slithered backward. The officer went to the back and he stepped forward.

In his last attempt to resist arrest, Mr. Thom was like a scorpion that runs into a tight spot in the baseboards where you can't squish it easily. There it clings, tightly squashing itself into a crevice, hoping you will be unable to see it or reach it or will become distracted or bored. But inevitably most scorpions that do this get squished and just as inevitably a big policeman yanked Mr. Thom from behind the massive pink concrete ice cream cone, and dragged him up the street while calling urgently on his radio for backup. While he was dragged away, Mr. Thom cursed and struggled uselessly against the officer's strong grip.

"Unhand me!" Mr. Thom ordered.

"This way, sir," said the policeman.

But this was probably not the finale of the fight. We only saw what happened in front of us. As our float pulled away, we all strained to see more of the fight which had managed to move up a side street and involved left-over members of the two groups who were still going at each other.

I played the music blindly. I was so amused I could barely see the notes, but I knew the notes by heart by then. Moses and I laughed so hard our brains and our mouths felt broken.

◆ ◆ ◆

Our float carried us back to the staging center where we drove in quietly. Most of the crowd had run down the street to see the big battle, and actually a lot of the people in the parade had done the same thing. Only a few stragglers drifted back to the Tough Cuss town center.

I glanced wistfully at the gift shop near the post office, thinking of the gang of pretty girls who'd been there.

Then I was stunned! They were there again! They'd gathered outside the shop window.

The float stopped and I packed my trombone faster than ever. The shuffling old Shriners were filtering politely down the risers to a single set of portable steps. I wasn't going to wait my turn that day!

"Hey! Where are you going?" Moses asked, but I ignored him.

I jumped off the side of the float, ran across the street and jammed the trombone in the luggage compartment of the bus. I took off in the direction of the Tough Cuss Gift Shoppe.

The shop lady was serving three people in front of me so it took forever for her to get to me. I was terrified that the bus would go without me!

"How much for a pair of those turquoise earrings?" I asked frantically when I reached the counter.

"Which earrings?" asked the saleslady, coldly.

"Doesn't matter. Any one of them will do."

"Well, these—"

"Yes! I'll take them! Please! Hurry!"

"Ten dollars," she said suspiciously, lifting the pair off the display.

I pulled out my wallet and paid her.

The saleslady crouched down to find a gift box.

"No need! I'll take them." I grabbed them off the counter and ran outside. I walked up to the group of girls. Think of the walk of a total blind jerk, but a brave jerk, wearing a red felt fez. I thrust the pair of earrings into the hands of the prettiest girl. Was she ever shocked!

"For you! You're beautiful!" I said, fleeing madly.

Before she could thank me, I was halfway back to the Shriner bus. I was the last to board, thumping up the bus steps, two at a time. The driver pulled a lever and shut the door behind me. "Glad you could join us," he said sarcastically.

I fought my way to our usual seat at the back. The Shriners were clinking plastic cups in the aisle, toasting the giant battle they had seen, and shouting to one another in complete and utter happiness. I had my back thumped and my shoulder squeezed several times.

"Do you know James, the attack of the I.O.O.B. on the Mountain Men was a spectacle which I shall never forget as long as I live. I'm only happy that I have lived long enough to see it," Moses said, when I plopped breathlessly in the bus seat beside him. "And where have you been, my little lost one?'

"Who's the mother hen now, huh? I had an important errand. I won't forget that battle either," I agreed, changing the subject.

"Oh, but it was wonderful, James. It was perfect, but I guess I shouldn't say that. No one should enjoy egregious violence."

"I don't even know what that means, but, come on, let's enjoy it," I said shamelessly.

"Okay, let's," agreed Moses, taking a big swig of what seemed to be a Black Russian.

"It was really boss. Do you think they'll all get arrested?"

"Maybe. And it couldn't have happened to a better group of jerks. Do you know, to me it was reminiscent of a fresco of Dante's Inferno I once saw," Moses continued. "Except there was a large black monster eating a naked man and giving birth to another in the fresco. Other than that, it was real similar."

"Really? That sounds interesting. Giving birth? I'll have to take your word for it. I don't even know what a fresco is."

"Look that up for yourself then. In an art history book. I don't know who did the one I'm thinking of, but look for the black devil. You'll get a redo of what you just saw. Amazing. You'll see why I compare it to this day."

Moses was full of these references to classy stuff. It made talking to him very interesting and educational, if not also a little confusing at times. It was hard to believe someone so fun-loving was also so knowledgeable about art and music. Greeks, Romans, Italians. On the long drive home, what Moses told me about that fresco of Dante's Inferno proves there was about the same amount of weird stuff, whipping and clubbing and cuffing and slapping, in the picture as what we witnessed that day. Knowing Moses Grand was like having a private tutor or something.

CHAPTER ELEVEN

I'd been offered drinks on the Shriner bus before, but it wasn't until the Quibovari parade, a year after I had started playing with the Shriner band—and a gas of year that was—that I broke down and drank several scotch and sodas.

What made me take to drink when I had refused to before? Well, I'll tell you. I found out something terrible, something scary and awful.

It happened like this: Moses met me on the bus that Saturday and right away I noticed that he seemed to have something important on his mind. After I got him his first drink, a scotch and soda, he came out with it.

"Do you remember when we were at that bullring? And that clown bothered you?"

"Yeah, sure, how could I forget? That was one of the scariest things that's ever happened to me."

"Well, they just arrested a man in clown costume. He had stabbed a boy, a fifteen year old, at a circus in Mexico. I recognized him as the man who was talking to you."

"What!"

"He wasn't a real clown. Like I told you that day. I knew that he wasn't. One of ours, I mean. I thought he might have come from the local Shriners."

"Oh shit!"

"Oh shit is right, James. You could have been his intended victim that day. It was awful quiet in that passageway before I showed up."

"Are you okay?" Moses asked when he saw that I was staring

into space and I didn't answer him.

"Not really," I replied.

"What you need is a stiff drink," Moses suggested.

For the first time, I agreed. I felt I ought to be blotto, as they say. I felt the world owed me a drink. The whole thing had me shaken to my core. I'd almost been murdered! And for once I wanted to get sloshed with my friend Moses. The idea that I had nearly been killed by that clown freaked me out, man. It was an awful feeling. If he had stabbed someone else, there was nothing to say he wouldn't have stabbed me. I might have been only moments away from death at the hands of that horrible clown. And the more I thought about it, the more I realized that he must have been inside the bathroom and I'd only missed him by moving so fast to get out of what I sensed was an unsafe place. I peed in the hallway, something I had not done since I was little, which would have horrified my parents, but if I'd gone into that bathroom I'd have been killed.

It called for a stiff drink, or two. I didn't care what. I just wanted to be completely drunk when the shock of what happened truly hit. I was only halfway admitting to myself that the creepy aggressive clown I'd talked to was probably the same one that murdered the boy. It was a frightening thing for me to think about.

Moses didn't force me to drink, but he didn't stop me either. When I went to get Moses another drink and the bartender offered me one, as always, I went ahead and took it. Several of the old musicians came by and slapped me on the shoulder as they could see me getting one for myself. They always wanted to create another drunk. I stumbled up the aisle, back to the seats I shared with Moses feeling rather elated at what I had done. I'd finally done something seriously bad.

I figured if I had this one drink I would be mostly sober by the time we rode in the parade and completely sober by the time we got back into town. After all, I'd taken a whole can of beer once from the refrigerator at home and it hadn't done much to my ability to function. This was a mistake. I misunderstood the effect different kinds of alcohol have. I'd never heard that different liquors had different amounts of alcohol.

Unfortunately, the first drink didn't affect me as much as I'd counted on. I thought if I was going to get hit by scotch I'd know it right away. Well, who knows, maybe the barkeeper watered mine down for the first one. I didn't keep my eye on him and over the past year, I'd asked for watered down ones for Moses. The result was I wanted a second right away, before the full amount of the liquor had reached me. I walked back and asked for another, and the bar keeper was perfectly happy to oblige.

◆ ◆ ◆

An unusual float in the Quibovari parade that day was called the Patriot-mobile. I'd never seen it before. When we were parking near our float that day, Moses told me it was built upon a large old truck chassis and had been decorated with wood and saguaro ribs lashed to it with crisscrossed wire and cord. It had a series of flag holders along its sides which were used to hold American and Arizona flags mounted in an alternating pattern. This rolling monstrosity had appeared in many Southern Arizona parades and was always sure to create little or no interest in the public. What people asked frequently upon seeing the Patriot-mobile was "What's that dumb thing supposed to be?"

I overheard the Shriners discussing the Patriot-mobile.

"Are the men in the back of the float freaks?" asked Milton II sarcastically.

"Who let that horrid pile of crap into the parade?" asked the ancient foul-mouthed flute player who sat several rows in front of me.

"It's been in Quibovari Days every year since I've been playing for the Shriners. That's been fifteen years. They built it on a 1931 Ford, I think," someone piped up.

"No, it were a Studebaker."

"He's right. Studebaker."

"Whatever it is underneath, the top is hideous."

"I agree."

"That is the crappiest looking parade float I have ever had the misfortune to have to look at. And be in a parade with," said the flute player.

"The people in this town pretend to like it."

"You're kidding."

By this time, I was feeling very drunk. I wasn't interested in the Patriot-mobile, or what truck bed it was built on, or whether it was unattractive. I can't even tell you who said all those bad things about the Patriot-mobile. I just wanted the world to stay still and my heart to stop pounding its way toward my throat.

"Moses," I said when we were seated on the float for ten minutes, "I feel real funny. I'm so drunk that I'm not sure I can play or stay on the float."

"Oh, god. Let's try to get you back to the bus..." Moses stood up and looked helplessly around.

"Ladies and Gentlemen, The Shriner Band!" shouted the announcer.

Just then the truck pulling our float lurched forward and the flat bed followed. I almost fainted from the jerking motion. The sky whirled above and the sun seemed to set in the east. Very rapidly. Moses told me later my head flopped on my shoulder and I slumped down in the chair.

"Don't worry," whispered Moses, "I'll cover for you. The guys know you drank and they won't hold it against you. Just don't vomit or something. Lean back in your chair or lie down."

The mention of vomiting made me think I might.

"Oh, I feel like vomiting!"

"What's wrong," asked Gluey.

"James is sick. Light headed?" Moses asked me.

"Very," I cried.

"Go down flat."

He didn't have to say it twice. I fell off the chair and lay on the plywood panels of the float as it started its journey down Quibovari Street to cheering crowds. Moses thought quickly, whipped off his vest and threw it over me so that I was partially covered and the crowd might not notice that I had passed out.

The route picked by the organizers of Quibovari Days followed Roosevelt Street, which was also the natural gully of Big Flood Gulch as it meandered through the town. It was one of the worst parades for the Shriner float because of the uneven and downward sweep of the parade route.

"Ladies and Gentlemen, the Copper State Conquistadores from Hell Canyon, Arizona!"

And then a minute later: "The Patriot-mobile from Rancho El Quibovari," said the proud voice of the announcer from the loudspeakers located throughout the parade route. The strange contraption known as The Patriot-mobile had only just crossed the parade start line. People thronged to the curb with bags of rock candy and toffee while saloons with names like Lucky Cuss and Sweet Tomorrow crowded over their shoulders like large uncles without a sense of humor.

"We welcome to our parade this year the very unique Patriot-mobile. We see this for the fifteenth time this year and it...amaze us here in the parade booth. A splendid sight to see on this great American day in Quibovari..."

The Patriot-mobile rolled down the crowded streets and its driver stared at the dusty steep route ahead, barely glancing left or right. Driving in parades was a huge responsibility and this parade had narrow streets and dangerous turns that he could hardly negotiate with this large ungainly machine.

Ranch troglodytes, hung off the float in various crazy attitudes, shouted things like "Wahoo!" and "Yee-ha!" Their shouting was distracting enough without the crowds and the animals as well. There were donkeys in front of this float and the driver had to keep his eyes on them at all times. In front of the donkeys were a bunch of conquistador guys and further ahead still, us, the Shriners.

"I don't think he knows how to turn the thing," said Moses, talking to me about the Patriot-mobile driver. "The whole crazy machine might just peel off into the crowd when he turns the wheel."

The driver kept the Patriot-mobile aimed for the center of the street and gave it lots of gas. He didn't want to stall the thing as he had done in that parade in New Mexico, and then create a horrible situation.

I rested for a while under Moses' vest as our float navigated the steep street and the band played without me. But when we neared the bottom of one sharp turn of the gulch, an overwhelming urge told me to stand up with the trombone in my hands.

The way Moses explains it, I came to a rigid upright position. Moses claimed he yelled for me to sit down, but I don't remember this. I staggered back against the poles which were installed along the side of the float and tore through some paper with my one arm flailing. I flipped backwards over the pole as neatly as any kid on a playground, flew out onto the street upside down and landed on my feet with my trombone still in my hands.

Moses figured what happened was the float did a small jerk and I lost my footing. He swore up and down that I should never worry that the thing happened because I was drunk. He claimed I would have fallen off anyway because of the way the float acted when it hit the turn of the street. In fact, Moses claimed I would have been much more greatly injured had I not been liquored up. He said everybody knew that drunks could take a bad fall and come out fine and I would have broken my neck if I hadn't been drunk when the float turned and lurched. Well, he might be right. I flew off and landed in the dirt road, completely uninjured.

I still had my trombone in my hand and he said it appeared I was bringing it to my lips and about to unlock the slide as though I thought I ought to keep playing. Some Conquistadores and their donkeys plodded by on either side of me.

A family friend heard from some other relatives of mine who live in town and who are gossiping jerks by the way, that I was drunk at the time of the accident. Big deal. And yes, I had had my second taste of alcohol, if I have to announce that to everyone as though I'm confessing and I am not even Catholic, I was confirmed a Congregationalist only a few years ago. (What a ridiculous ceremony that was and I hadn't been baptized so the minister did the baptism hoo-haa and pronounced my middle name wrong in front of the whole congregation! James Ed-witch, he said and Ginny and Gertrude shrieked for hours and said I had been baptized a witch in church! Junk like that happens to me all the time.) It's not like I got arrested for drinking or for anything. Damn. I wasn't arrested at all for any of it. Possibly the scotch and soda was what made me fall off backwards from the Shriner float—I'll admit it—when the float turned following the path of the Big Gulch in Quibovari. I'm certainly willing to concede that point, but not much more as far as thinking that I did the whole thing. I don't remember it too clearly, but the big facts I have right, because the whole thing was written up in some newspapers, including our local paper. A junky rag, by the way. It's the shock of it all that has made me forget the details. And none of this is saying that I don't feel bad about what happened, because in a way I probably do feel a little guilty.

So you need to know an additional fact. In this little town of Quibovari, there stood an adobe that President Teddy Roosevelt had once momentarily strolled into after departing the train, or you could say that he rolled into it. (He was a hefty guy I hear, weighing over 300 pounds.) What happened then was he stubbed his toe on an adobe brick, barreled over to the bar, and used the spittoon for a brief, but historic, moment of important presidential spitting. The whole scene is probably pretty big in the scheme of the world or something, and way more important than me, of course. No kidding! I think he was a groovy guy and if he went into a building in Arizona even to spit once, then that building ought to be preserved for posterity and all that. Now all there is left of the place is the staircase and a bronze historical plaque with the dates and a funny silhouette of President Roosevelt's face, double chins and all.

The Roosevelt Adobe, as it was known, was once a historical place but now it's a pile of rubble, broken boards, plaster, and mud. I know it's a crying shame. Moses said it was a shame, a crying shame, but I ought not to blame myself, and he was there to see the whole thing that happened. He wouldn't have let me off if I did something wrong either. He was the type of old geezer who takes right and wrong very seriously. He was a straight and honorable fellow. Not like me.

Well, the damn driver of the Patriot-mobile float drove that horrible thing cheerfully through the jam packed, narrow streets of Quibovari. He probably loved the old towns like Quibovari with their shabby adobe homes and rotted wood facades lining the main streets. I'll bet he liked the way the dusty little windows, painted white, showed fancy lace curtains and odd bottle collections of old patent medicines in crazy glass. Most likely, he felt a part of the parade and the festivities and a big smile grew across his face, which he shone out the window like a beacon of happiness at the people watching the Patriot-mobile ride by. He wanted them to enjoy the patriotic sight of so many flags flying together, the Arizona and the American flag, symbols of this great nation, flapping in the Quibovari breeze, and he hoped the people on the float weren't acting too crazy in the back of the truck and disgracing the flags, though from the ruckus he heard he had every reason to believe they were behaving in their usual outrageous fashion, although he couldn't see them even if he strained his neck out the window. Besides, that was dangerous when you had to drive in a parade.

Suddenly the Patriot-mobile saw me standing in the middle of the steep street.

Moses said when I flew off the Shriner float the old guy who played percussion with an open mouth had his mouth drop further open. He stared at what he saw, which was me doing a flip in the air and landing in the parade route on my feet. As the Shriner float drove forward, Moses and most of the band swung their heads around to check their impressions again. Yeah, sure enough James Sauerbaugh had flown off the float and landed in the street and James was going on with his music as though nothing had happened. A couple of scotch on the rocks will do that.

For my part, I was just as stunned to see the Patriot-mobile. The awful machine loomed above me like some hideous monster, closing in for the kill. I was about to be run over by an insane-looking float.

When I saw the awful Patriot-mobile my mind was filled with fear. Immediately I began searching for a way back onto the Shriner float. I blundered forward two steps toward the disappearing Shriners, hearing Moses shouting: "Watch out! James? My little lost one!"

But there was it, the pride of the ranching community, that old Patriot-mobile rolling down on me, and all I could see was a mass of flags, and sticks and hay bale benches, manned by the freakish ranch hands in what was probably their only day off the ranch in six months, whooping and hollering for all it was worth, as this crazy machine bore down in its highly twisty and dangerously downhill wind. I do remember Moses hollering, "James, James, get to the side!"

Later Moses laughed about saying that. He knew I was so drunk there was absolutely no way that I was going to be able to move.

The driver, seeing me in the street, swerved to avoid killing me. He plowed into the Roosevelt Adobe.

Almost in slow motion, the Patriot-mobile collided full force with the old building which once had entertained Teddy Roosevelt, and was the state's tallest adobe building, a massive old mud structure.

The collision was at fairly slow speed, but had the force of a higher speed impact due to the decrepit state of the building. I suppose that truck hit at just the right spot to cause a total collapse. It was unlucky the way the thing exploded.

Shoot, the impact that resulted between the two objects was pretty sad to watch, but it was undoubtedly theatrical, of the nature of a good mine cave-in or an avalanche or a train wreck. A great deal of noise resulted first. Shopkeepers dashed out their doors at the boom. The sound was huge with greater volume than had been heard in the town of Quibovari since they were mining in the old Turkey Vulture Mine, which had closed in 1938. The bang sent a flock of pigeons soaring out over the desert. A flock of migratory Sandhill cranes, wintering on the stinky sewage pond to the west of Quibovari, took flight and began their migration back to Kansas or Siberia or wherever they came from like good Arizona snow birds. Several old men crossed themselves and looked to the sky for balls of fire falling. Everyone else tried to see where the sound had come from and what they saw astounded them.

Splintering wood flew skyward in an explosive display of a collision's ability to pulverize objects. It looked as though a stick of dynamite had been planted in the roof. The boards shot into the air, flipping in a way that made the crowd fear for their lives, but thank goodness every bit of that lumber landed harmlessly on the roofs of adjacent buildings.

The old truck buried itself into the tall adobe brick side of the old building like an ugly terrier after a rat. The Patriot-mobile shoved itself in as though it really meant business. And it met little resistance.

Then the famous old building caved in. Shoot, I have heard many people talk about the wonder of Niagara Falls, but they had nothing on the privileged people who got to see the Roosevelt Adobe, the tallest mud structure in Arizona, collapse. A rain of mud, a wall of mud came down. I might have been pretty drunk, but I could appreciate what I was seeing. It was dramatic. Many in the crowd groaned and gasped at the sight of the tallest adobe structure in Arizona reducing itself to a loose brown dusty rubble. Its monumental history went down with it in a rapid descent to nothingness, the collapse being quick and therefore somewhat painless, but very definite. It was as though the whole edifice was built of dust particles coaxed together temporarily and returning to a more sustainable position flat on the ground.

Suddenly, the dry mud which had shot down, ricocheted and filled the turquoise sky. The huge plume of rust colored dust rose into the sky above Quibovari.

My drunken eyes scanned the old adobe building in astonishment. Another thunderous clap sounded. The air filled with muddy dust which fell in every direction on the screaming crowd. The dust-covered people nearby shouted and cursed and tasted the dust on their faces. Kids had dusty faces, old folks had dusty faces. The parade participants, many of whom were already strangely dressed, were now coated with a thin layer of dirt.

And the Patriot-mobile driving into the side of the wall did not kill a single individual, thank goodness, but mostly filled their faces and hair with a soft powder of ruddy dirt. The poor occupants of the building, two local historians, stumbled out, dusty but unharmed. Scrambling one-by-one out of the wrecked float which was embedded in the adobe debris, the driver and the troglodytes escaped the torrent of adobe, old boards and tin ceiling tiles. And these covered victims came coughing out, bursting out of the rubble. Policemen ran to the aid of the poor people on the Patriot-mobile and anyone else who had not escaped the collapsing landmark. In a few seconds a fire alarm sounded. A fire engine began racing to the scene along with the town's only paramedic van. People ran toward the building but stopped when they saw the rubble.

Those on the Patriot-mobile fell about the sidewalk joining the other victims of the accident, all of whom were covered with the same coating of brown mud. Combined with several old conquistadors—guard with pikes, flower-laden donkeys, hysterical parade officials, and tuba players, the general disorder and piquancy of the scene made a fabulous wreck.

It was toward this crazy scene that Moses ran pell-mell

through the startled and screaming crowd, running with his heart in his mouth, he told me later, craning his neck above the crowd in order to catch a glimpse of the victims and figure out which of the dust covered figures might be me.

As Moses drew closer the coughing figures were clearer. It was like talking to cocoa covered people, whose eyes looked out, but whose features were hidden in the thick layer of pulverized adobe. I stood near the middle of the awe-struck crowd. It was puzzling to him, he said, to find me. The dust clearly covered most of the people on the street, but I was only lightly dusted.

One of the cocoa powder covered men took the lens off his camera. Before Moses could slip me off into the crowd, my photograph was taken.

And the accompanying newspaper article read "boy in street with trombone causes float to swerve into historic structure, Roosevelt Adobe, Quibovari, Arizona."

CHAPTER TWELVE

My parents went ape over what happened. Ah, man, at first I thought it was nothing important, funny and pretty cool, until my mother called a halt to me being in the Shriner band. When I came home drunk that day, and my face was in the newspapers the next day as the boy who'd nearly been hit by a float, she and my old man asked me a lot of questions about what happened and when it was clear that I had gotten drinks directly from the Shriners, they decided they didn't want me playing with the band any more. Being with so many adult men was the problem, Mom figured. I guess when my old man was talking about all the fun he'd had in bands when he had snuck into bars, he wasn't exactly being straight with himself about under-age drinking. He wasn't so happy when he faced me being drunk. So I didn't go with the Shriners to finish out the year of parades and circuses. My old man stopped my lessons with Gluey, too.

Several nosy family friends phoned Mom about it, although I never heard any of these calls myself, but Mom yakked about how awful it was when I got home from school. I like to imagine the calls, in my head, and I think they went something like this: "Hello, Barbara? This is Flo for the four hundredth time this week, wanting to phone you casually, oh, just to bug all of you out of your tiny little minds, and find out for sure what you're going to do about James Eldritch. No one, I mean absolutely no one, can believe that it really was your boy, James Eldritch, who caused the destruction of that historic building."

"Oh yes, Florence. That was our good little boy, our wonderful little Jimmie Wimmie," says my mother.

"We want to make sure you're doing something to James. How about a torture session or something, huh?"

"Sure, we plan that for tomorrow afternoon."

"Well, I hope you are going to stretch him on the rack?"

"Absolutely! While watching Merv Griffin."

Yeah, yeah. I kept telling them over and over that they shouldn't have been bothered by phone calls from ridiculous people who were just calling up to casually bug us and wanting to know if it really was me that destroyed what they called a world-famous Arizona landmark. Let me give you a hint, nothing in Arizona is world-famous or a landmark. Except maybe the Grand Canyon and that's just a hole in the ground.

I might have had my reputation besmirched by what happened. And tainted. And dishonored. And tarnished (hey, that's cool, sort of tying in with the band instrument thing!) Despoiled even. I might have been despoiled in everyone's eyes because of my drunken accident. Well, okay, despoiled might be going a bit too far with the story because dammit, I didn't manage to lose my virginity once in the whole thing and I really, really could have used that happening, let me tell you, as I face down registering for the draft soon and hope I don't have to be shipped off to Vietnam if my number comes up or if I do I hope I can get into college and get a bunch of draft deferments until the war is over. But if none of that happens and I get drafted, I wish I had been despoiled at least once. Notice I did use all my English vocabulary words there, besmirched and all that, so, holy crap, I'm picking up some cool shit in high school!

But I wasn't mortified and my head is not going to get messed with. No siree, Bob. Forces That Be, hit the road. My head remains my own! Can you dig it?

Well, I'm not particularly bugged by what I did, but that's not to say I'm proud. I think President Roosevelt was a groovy guy and if he went into a saloon in Arizona even to spit once, then that saloon ought to be preserved for posterity and all that. Now there's only the staircase and that plaque with silhouette of President Roosevelt's face, double chins and all, like a buncha of western buttes or plateaus running off his face at the bottom. The Roosevelt Adobe, as it was known, was once a historical place but now it's a pile of goddamn rubble, broken boards, plaster, and mud. Shoot, I know it's a crying shame. Moses said it was, but he said I ought not to blame myself, and he was there to see the whole thing happen. He wouldn't have let me off if I did something wrong, either. He was the type of old geezer who takes right and wrong very seriously. He was a straight and honorable fellow. Not like me.

Anyway, I have to tell you the terrible truth now, and get right to it.

Two parades later, that is, two parades after I fell off the float and the Roosevelt Adobe was destroyed, Moses got more crocked than usual while he was with the band and his blood alcohol level reached the danger level. He died on the Shriner bus. Before they even got him to a hospital.

Moses always asked me to get him drinks when we were together and I never argued but went right along with what he wanted over and over, again and again.

I can only guess that Moses took my trouble pretty hard and he must have had a few too many on the next trips. Of course when I was with him I was asking the bartender to make them so that the alcohol ran a little on the lean side, but once he was getting them himself that probably ended, I don't know anyone else who would have taken that on, and he probably was making sure that they had plenty of liquor in them himself.

I wish I had been there. Maybe I could have stopped him from drinking so much or seen what was happening faster, because I was his helper all those times before. Maybe it wouldn't have made any difference. I'm glad I wasn't there when he died, if he was going to die on the bus.

I didn't even find out about the death myself. My mom read it in the obituary article in the newspaper first and then mentioned that it was a Shriner who died. She thought I'd mentioned the name Moses Grand.

It was hard to read about his life in a newspaper that way

after we'd had so many fun adventures together, and even more than I've told you. I wished I could have stayed with him to the end, but it wasn't to be.

I drove myself to his funeral. First time driving alone.

It was a Jewish funeral, a couple days after he died. With a rabbi. The whole scene.

Gluey was there and he talked to me for a few minutes, but I don't remember a thing he said. How could I? I was crying about as hard as a person is able.

That small obituary which my mother had clipped out of the local paper with Moses' face under the fez looks at me now with the same crazy Santa Claus smile. The obituary was all about his devotion to the Shriners and kids in hospitals. It said his second son, named Abe, had died at the age of seventeen. Boy, when I read that it hit me hard. I thought it was strange when he started calling me "his little lost one." Maybe it wasn't me that was lost, but his real kid who'd been my age when he died.

What am I gonna do now? What's my big life goal besides not going to Vietnam? Well, I'm gonna do good deeds for kids, mostly, somehow. And this spring I have a little plan for myself. If I do my research, my friend Scott and I might just graduate from high school and join up with that nudist camp I once heard about from Moses. The one in the canyon near Highway 242 in Santa Cruz County. They could probably use a blindish guy who plays circus music on the trombone.

ABOUT THE AUTHOR

Lorraine Ray

Visit   amazon.com/author/
lorraine-ray to find more books
by Lorraine.

Contact   at
lorraine.ray00@gmail.com

BOOKS BY THIS AUTHOR

Last Days In The Desert

An outrageous party leads to a day of hungover misadventures for three undergrads who had hoped to shut down their rental home and get back their security deposit before leaving town. Instead, they have to fix a gaping hole in an adobe wall and rid themselves of unwanted graduation "presents," both the result of the uproarious party. A zany romp of high and low comedy.

Familiar Artifacts

Attention, suspense fans! These twelve tales contain witches, liars, and murderers. They are specially crafted to jolt you out of the mundane. Proceed with caution!

Juan And Willy

Who hasn't dreamed of finding gold? After Juan and Willy are fired from their jobs as car handlers at a dealership, a desire for gold possesses them. Locating a lost mine, however, means they have to outsmart a kid, a huge challenge for this pair. With an idea of where some lost gold might be, they search for a truck with an intact transmission that isn't full of feral cats. Of course, abandoned mines aren't safe places either, a fact especially true for these sorry, but sweet, friends.

Dastardly

Impoverished author Marc Viglietti languishes in his job at a rodeo parade museum while dreaming of fame and fortune from the ridiculous vampire westerns he can't stop penning.

I Want My Own Brain

Spend a weekend with Stephanie Falls, age eight, at her doting grandparents' home. Trapped in their mansion full of creepy taxidermy and unappreciated Native American art, Stephanie plays with everything she sees, breaking and mutilating quite a few objects. An excursion to march in a mountain man parade ends badly for Grandpa Drummond when Stephanie torments an important parade organizer. Despite her appalling behavior, Stephanie's antics inspire Aunt Helen to begin life anew with zeal and confidence.

Made in the USA
Las Vegas, NV
31 January 2024

85130611R00100